THE MARQUESS MATCH

LOVE'S A GAME
BOOK THREE

VALERIE BOWMAN

JUNE THIRD ENTERPRISES, LLC

Digital edition ISBN: 978-1-960015-29-7

Print edition ISBN: 978-1-960015-30-3

Book Cover Design © Lyndsey Llewellen at Llewellen Designs.

She's a walking scandal
Clare Handleton was ruined years ago and has borne the consequences ever since. Branded as "Scandalton" by the *ton*, she has long since stopped caring about Society's fickle rules. Now, at twenty-nine, she's mastered the art of slipping past her mother's scrutiny, appearing unfazed by it all. But when the dangerously handsome Marquess of Trentham crosses her path, he stirs something she thought long buried.

He's a scandal magnet
Ashford Drake, the Marquess of Trentham, is the very definition of devil-may-care. He's made it known, even in the presence of the King, that marriage is off the table for him. Why would he want to continue his hated father's legacy? So when his sister's intriguing friend catches his eye, matrimony is the last thing on his mind.

Have they both met their match?
Thrown together during the London autumn season, Clare and Ash's paths cross at a notorious pleasure club. They strike a deal: no strings attached, no emotions involved. But what happens when breaking their own rules becomes inevitable?

CHAPTER ONE

Surrey, October 1818, The Duke of Southbury's Country Estate

Wearing nothing but her chemise and a silk dressing gown that clung to her body like mist, Lady Clare Handleton moved soundlessly down the dim corridor. The chill of the marble staircase seeped into her bare feet as she descended, her fingers trailing absently along the polished banister. The weight of silence pressed against her, heavy and familiar. Darkness swallowed the grand foyer, broken only by the pale glow of moonlight spilling through the high windows. Her breath was steady, her pulse an old, familiar drum against her ribs.

She had grown accustomed to moving in the dark, and she knew these halls. She was in her dearest friend's country home, after all. Meredith Brooks and her husband, Griffin, the Duke of Southbury, were two of her only friends. They had stayed loyal when all others had long since disappeared.

The grand foyer stretched before her, awash in silver moonlight, its vastness making her feel small. But she ignored the sensation, as she always did. Pushing forward, she made her way down another long corridor and slipped through Southbury's study door with the ease of someone who had spent years mastering the art of going unnoticed.

Not that she cared whether she was noticed any longer.

She closed the door with careful precision and crossed to the sideboard. The crystal decanter gleamed in the soft light, and without hesitation, she lifted it, pouring two fingers of the duke's finest brandy into a heavy glass.

The first sip burned, a slow, spreading warmth winding through her. She exhaled, long and leisurely, letting her head tip back as the tension in her limbs melted away. Her unbound blonde hair cascaded past her waist, and for the first time that day, she allowed herself the illusion of peace.

Until a voice shattered it.

"Couldn't sleep?"

It was a deep, male voice. Rich, husky, sinful. Unmistakably amused.

Clare didn't startle. She had mastered the art of concealment years ago—never let them see, never let them know.

She forced her eyes open, turning toward the voice with deliberate slowness, as though she had all the time in the world. Another trick she'd mastered over the last eleven years.

The study was steeped in shadow, but she knew instantly who he was. And it wasn't the duke.

The voice was too smooth, too practiced in the ways of troublemaking.

She took a step forward, and as she did, the moonlight shifted, revealing him.

Ah. So it *was* him.

Plenty of trouble. Or could be, depending on how this conversation unfolded.

Ashford Drake, the Marquess of Trentham and Meredith's older brother, sat there. His tall, muscled form sprawled with the kind of ease that suggested he belonged anywhere he chose. The sharp cut of his cheekbones, the knowing tilt of his lips—everything about him radiated mischief, barely concealed beneath a veneer of aristocratic boredom.

And damn him, he was watching her with a look she *felt*.

"You?" she asked, lifting her glass to her lips again, meeting his gaze without hesitation.

Trentham unfolded himself from the chair with the effortless grace of a predator stretching after a long, indulgent rest. In a few unhurried strides, he stood before her. Close enough that she could smell the faint trace of his expensive cologne and something even more arousing beneath it—something undeniably *male*.

"Something like that," he murmured, his voice roughened by amusement.

Before she could react, he plucked the glass from her fingers, the heat of his touch lingering against her skin. He lifted it to his lips, taking a slow, deliberate sip as he held her gaze.

"This is Southbury's finest brandy," he noted, his voice all lazy observation.

"I know," she replied. "That's why I wanted it."

A slow grin curved his lips. "Does he know you're here?"

"Does he know *you're* here?" she countered, arching a brow at him. She'd long ago stopped answering questions simply because they were asked. Another art.

Trentham laughed—low, quiet, and far too pleased.

"Don't you know?" she mused, stepping just a fraction closer, her voice dipped in the kind of defiance that had earned her her reputation. "You're speaking to Lady Clare Handleton, better known as Scandalton." *There*. That should tell him how little she cared for rules.

"Oh, I'm well aware of who you are," he murmured, tilting his head. "But that doesn't explain why you're here. A woman whose name is already whispered in scandal should be a touch more careful, don't you think?"

She eyed him up and down. Oh, no. Not him. *He* couldn't be smug. The man was far from a saint himself.

But let him think her reckless. Let him think her ruined beyond repair. "Your thought process is flawed," she informed him. "Because one of the very few perks of being well and truly ruined is the freedom to do precisely as I please." She lifted her chin in the air and narrowed her eyes at him. She took another sip of brandy.

Trentham pressed his lips together, as if suppressing a smile. *He liked that.* She could see it in the way his gray eyes sparked with something dangerously close to admiration. She had a feeling he'd only said what he had to see her reaction. She would never back down in the face of judgement. She had far too much experience with it.

"What are the other perks?" he asked. His voice was softer now, more curious than mocking.

She blinked. A small crease formed between her brows. "Pardon?"

"You said one of the few perks," he reminded her. "I'm intrigued. What are the others?"

For the first time that night, Clare hesitated. He had caught her off guard. And worse—he had amused her.

A slow, knowing smile played at the corner of her lips.

"You're very interested in my ruination, Lord Trentham."

His eyes darkened slightly, the humor still there but laced with something heavier. Something unreadable. "I'm interested in a great many things."

She refused to let herself react to the way he said it. Instead, she reached for her glass again, but he pulled it away, held it just out of reach. Then he took another sip before handing the glass back to her. Their fingers brushed—brief, fleeting, sending an unwanted shiver up her spine. She could only hope he hadn't noticed. That sort of information in the hands of a man like Trentham could be dangerous. It occurred to her that she'd never seen him like this. They'd never been alone together. Ash was normally the center of attention at every party. The devil-may-care charmer who held court with plenty of brandy and plenty of beautiful women fluttering about him. And Clare was the precise opposite. She rarely appeared in Society these days. And when she did, she'd made it a habit to stick to the sidelines, the shadows, where fewer people would see her. Where fewer whispers would start.

It was off-putting, being the sole focus of his attention here alone in the dark. Off-putting and…exhilarating.

"You're down here in the middle of the night," he continued, tilting his head. "Which tells me you have *some* regard for propriety, or you'd be here in the middle of the day."

Her smile faltered, just for a second. He was astute. Perhaps more astute than she'd ever given him credit for. The man was beautiful, tall and muscled, with thick dark hair and steely gray eyes. A sharp jaw and a mouth so perfect it looked as if it had been carved from stone. A man so handsome was not usually clever as well. She supposed it had been a fantasy of hers, knowing him all these years, and assuming he was little more than a feast for the eyes.

"You could be here in the middle of the day," he said, watching her. "Why aren't you?"

That was an excellent question.

One that had little to do with scandal—and everything to do with the truth she wasn't willing to speak aloud.

Because it wasn't the thrill of rebellion that kept her awake at night.

It was loneliness. It was restlessness.

And it was the man standing right in front of her.

The Marquess of Trentham—the one man who had always made her feel something other than numb.

But she wouldn't tell him that. She refused to.

Instead, she took another sip of brandy and let the slow burn of it fill the silence between them. Then she looked up at him with a slow, wicked smile.

"Because, my lord," she murmured, handing him the glass, "some things are best done in the dark."

CHAPTER TWO

Ash shifted his stance, letting the cool weight of the crystal tumbler rest against his fingers as he studied her.

Clare Handleton.

His sister Meredith's closest friend and the woman every debutante in London had been warned not to become.

She stood before him, golden hair tumbling in wild, untamed waves down her back, her light-pink dressing gown slipping off one bare shoulder, revealing a thin white chemise beneath. She should have looked vulnerable like that, standing barefoot in the duke's study, drinking stolen brandy in the middle of the night. But vulnerability wasn't something Clare wore. No, she draped herself in defiance like the finest silk, her chin lifted, her mouth curved in an insouciant smile.

Ash had always known Clare Handleton was trouble.

She wore it like a crown, carried it with the kind of effortless grace that made people forget she hadn't chosen this reputation—it had been thrust upon her. She'd been ruined eleven years ago. Ruined and shunned. A terrible fate for a debutante. And instead of trying to claw her way back into Society's good graces, she had simply shrugged, smirked, and made sure she had the last laugh. Which meant she had courage. Courage and an insolent streak. Who wouldn't admire such a woman?

Scandalton, the *ton* had named her.

She didn't mind that moniker either, apparently. She'd just reminded him about it, actually, as if she couldn't care any less.

Even now, standing in the dim glow of moonlight, barefoot and draped in nothing but silk and shadows, she looked completely at ease. As if this were her kingdom, and he was the one trespassing.

God help him, he liked that about her.

He liked a lot about her, actually. Her attitude, her demeanor, her…beauty. And she truly was a beauty. Tall, lithe, with blonde hair and dark eyes that shimmered with amusement and sparked with defiance. He'd never been alone with her before. Never had reason to. But tonight he was noticing her in a completely different way. That nearly see-through shift she was wearing didn't help matters. Her body looked as if it was made for a man's hands, and her face was equally gorgeous, with high cheekbones and long black lashes.

And despite her reputation, Meredith would not be so close to her if she wasn't a good sort. Loyal. Steadfast. Clever. And witty. All things his sister valued in her friends. All things Meredith was herself.

Ash eyed Clare up and down. It was a pity what had happened to her. And damn unfair if you asked him. Women couldn't make the same mistakes men did. The consequences were far different.

Everyone in the *ton* knew what had happened. Clare had been ruined, discarded, left to rot in the margins of polite

Society. Some whispered in pity, others in scorn. But Clare? She only ever smiled in that slow, wicked way, as if she were in on a joke no one else understood.

But Ash understood. He was only too familiar with the disapproval of the *ton*. Only he'd courted it. Wanted it. To the great concern of his beloved sister, he'd created a reputation for himself that left much to be desired. If Clare was a walking scandal, then Ash was a scandal magnet.

Yes, he and Scandalton had something in common all right. And here they were, alone in the dark, drinking stolen liquor like two people who didn't belong anywhere else. And honestly, he couldn't remember the last time he'd been so intrigued by a woman.

Clare lifted her gaze to his, her eyes glinting like polished amber in the moonlight. "Don't you know my story, Trentham? I'm damaged goods."

Ash took a deliberate sip from the glass he'd stolen from her, savoring the way her lips parted slightly in surprise. "You're nothing of the sort," he said, voice low and certain. "And I know the Earl of Marsden. He's the biggest ass I've ever met."

Something flickered in her eyes. Not gratitude, not exactly. More like...acknowledgment. A sharp glint of respect, maybe.

"That sounds like him," she murmured. "Though I wasn't aware that everyone knew his identity."

"The ladies may not, but I assure you the gentlemen do, and we're all itching to club Marsden in the head given the opportunity."

"*Really?* I never knew. I'd like to join that hunting party."

She was so damn close. Her breath brushed his skin, laced with brandy and something softer underneath—something sweet he couldn't name but suddenly wanted to taste.

Ash exhaled slowly, willing himself to keep his hands right where they were. Off her.

If Meredith hadn't been hosting this house party, Clare wouldn't have been invited. If Meredith weren't the sister of a marquess and a duchess in her own right, half the ladies in attendance would have refused to come, just to avoid breathing the same air as Lady Clare.

But Meredith was Meredith. And Scandalton was Scandalton.

It would have been easier if she were a naïve, wide-eyed debutante. If she batted her lashes and blushed prettily at his attention, like the rest of the ladies in attendance at this house party that his sister had insisted he attend. Because then he could have stolen a kiss and convinced himself it was harmless.

But Clare wasn't innocent.

And for that very reason, he would never dishonor her like that.

Not her.

Not after what she'd been through, after the way the disapproving *ton* had already stripped her of everything and left her with nothing but her pride and that sharp-edged smile.

Damn it all though—he *wanted* to kiss her.

"I'm sorry for what happened to you," he said, his voice rougher than he intended. "The earl wasn't worth it."

A crack of laughter escaped her, sharp and unexpected. "How well I know it."

She turned, crossing the room to the darkened window. Her fingers glanced along the pane.

Ash watched her, the tension in his chest settling into something heavier.

She wasn't a woman who needed apologies. She'd been

through hell, and she had come out the other side, chin lifted, daring the world to try again.

But that didn't mean she didn't deserve one.

There was only a sip of brandy left in the glass. He downed it before stepping toward the sideboard. "Refill?"

She shook her head. "I should get back to bed. Mama sometimes checks in on me. If I'm not there, she'll assume the worst."

Something about that struck him harder than it should have. The thought of being watched, judged, found lacking. He knew it well. He hadn't felt it in years, but he knew it.

And he hated that she still had to feel it.

She moved past him toward the door, and before he could think better of it, his hand shot out, fingers closing gently around her wrist.

She froze. Turned her head slowly, her sharp, assessing eyes locking onto his. "Yes?"

Ash didn't let go. "Meet me here again," he said, surprising even himself. "Tomorrow night. Another drink."

Where the hell those words had come from, he had no idea. All he knew was that for the first time in years—hell, perhaps ever—he was looking forward to something.

She had to say yes. She had to.

Her gaze narrowed. "You think I'll be an easy conquest, my lord?" Her voice was light, teasing, but underneath it was something jagged. Something raw. "The once-used woman couldn't possibly refuse?"

His grip tightened—not enough to hurt, just enough to make sure she was listening. "Nothing like that," he said, fiercer than he'd meant to. "I promise it'll just be drinks. Just talking."

And he meant it.

That was what shocked him the most. He actually wanted to talk to her.

Clare studied him for a long, stretched-out moment. Then, slowly, she smiled. The kind of smile that made men make mistakes.

"Pity that," she murmured, the edges of her lips curving slightly in the smallest semblance of a grin.

Then, before he could react, she slipped free and disappeared into the darkened corridor.

Ash stood there, staring after her, bemused.

Pity that?

Did that mean she wanted more than just talking? She hadn't answered him. Would she come back?

He arched a brow and refilled the empty glass. There was only one way to find out.

CHAPTER THREE

"Clare? Are you listening?" Meredith's voice cut through the loud voices in the breakfast room the next morning.

She glanced over at her friend and forced a smile to her lips. "What was that?" she asked, proving undeniably that she had *not* been listening.

"I asked if you would like another scone," Meredith replied.

"Oh, yes, please. I'd like as many scones as possible," Clare said with a laugh, holding up her plate while Meredith plunked another scone upon it. Then she pushed the pot of cream toward her.

The food here was excellent, far better than what she and Mama had in the countryside. It was one of the reasons Clare had agreed to attend this house party. That and the fact that the whole purpose for the party had intrigued her from the moment Meredith had conceived of it. They were all here for one purpose and one purpose alone—to find a wife for Ash.

Oh, Clare had no illusions that *she* would be the chosen bride. Far from it. At nine and twenty, in addition to being a scandal-ridden ruin, she was a confirmed spinster, but it didn't keep her from morbid curiosity.

Ash had been a dashing figure in her life for over ten years now, ever since she and Meredith had become close friends during their debuts. He was always up to something, always the subject of an interesting tale. Once, Ash had famously announced to the King that he would never take a wife. And his exploits through the years certainly seemed to reinforce his claim. He was as scandal-ridden as Clare herself. Though as a man and a peer, he could get away with it.

And he never seemed to give a toss what rules he broke or what Society thought of it. They were cut from the same cloth, the two of them. She'd always known it. But last night had been the first time she'd had a chance to see it so closely. There had been a comradery between them last night, unspoken though it may have been. She'd felt it…and she guessed Ash had felt it too.

"Will you go riding with us later?" Meredith asked, causing Clare to pause in adding a ridiculous amount of cream to her scone.

She nearly choked. "Certainly *not*. I highly doubt the other young ladies and their mothers would appreciate my presence."

"I don't see why not," Meredith replied, rubbing a hand atop her expanding belly. Meredith was expecting her first child in February. This house party had been planned to take place before her confinement. She was in a race against time to find a bride for her unwilling brother. "Given my condition, I'll be in the open carriage. You may ride with me."

Clare reached out and patted her friend's hand. Meredith was fierce and loyal and wonderful. Clare was fortunate to have such a steadfast friend. But even Meredith's patronage couldn't keep the debutantes and their mothers from whispering behind their hands and their fans when Clare was around.

Even now, as they sat at the breakfast table, there were multiple pairs of eyes trained on her. Meredith didn't always notice, but Clare never missed it. She'd learned to live with the jibes and the gossip over the years. Had even learned to pretend to ignore it all. But she'd never learned how to keep it from bothering her.

Which was one reason her encounter with Ash last night in Griffin's study had so thoroughly surprised her. First, she was not aware that Ashford Drake even knew her name, let alone was "well aware" of who she was. When he'd said those words, she'd nearly melted to the floor in a puddle. And then he'd gone on to apologize to her for how she'd been treated by the *ton* and even added a bit of scorn for Marsden.

It had all been quite shocking, really. But none of it was as shocking as his proposal that they meet again…tonight.

She'd tossed and turned all night, unable to sleep for thinking about it. She'd challenged him, asking him if he thought she would be an easy conquest. Which honestly wasn't fair. But she'd learned through the years that most men she encountered in dark rooms alone were quite willing, if not eager, to present her with a scandalous proposal.

For all that Ash was known for his outrageous behavior, Clare had no indication that he was a lout. Meredith adored him, and the only conduct Clare had seen from him through the years had been nothing but honorable, if high-spirited. Still, she had to be certain that he wasn't asking her to return, hoping for a quick swive in the study. Because as handsome and charming as he was, *that* certainly wasn't going to happen.

Not that it wasn't tempting.

He'd surprised her further by insisting that he only wanted to talk to her. No one wanted to talk to her. Ever.

Meredith, Griffin, Griffin's younger sister, Gemma, and Gemma's new husband, Lucian, the Duke of Grovemont, were her only real friends. But Ash had seemed truly sympathetic last night.

It made her want to see him again. It made her want to talk to him. Only she must tread carefully. Under her mother's watchful eye, any slight misstep was cause for dramatics, and Mama had a penchant for waking in the middle of the night and checking in on her daughter. An exceedingly unpleasant and unfortunate habit.

Clare sighed and took another bite from her scone. As enticing as it was to contemplate another late-night, brandy drinking session with Ash, she had best not tempt fate. Her reputation had not survived her first scandal. A second one would be certain to ruin her forever.

CHAPTER FOUR

Ash couldn't remember the last time he'd spent such a restless day. He'd done everything expected of a man in his position—gone riding across the property with the other gentlemen in the morning, endured a tedious luncheon on the veranda with the entire party, taken an afternoon drink with Southbury in his study, and even walked alone through the orchards in a desperate attempt to shake the growing impatience inside him.

None of it helped.

By the time dinner arrived, he was in a foul mood, though he hadn't fully admitted to himself why.

Then he realized *she* wasn't there.

"Lady Clare will not be joining us this evening," Meredith had said casually as they walked into the dining room. "She's feeling unwell."

A megrim, she had called it.

He hadn't believed it for a second.

Clare Handleton was not a woman who retired early.

He had spent the evening feeling absurdly irritated at her absence, sipping his wine too fast, barely hearing the conversation around him. When he finally escaped to the study, he told himself it *wasn't* because he was hoping she would be here.

And yet, here he was. He'd waited for too long. Far longer than he'd ever waited for anyone in his life, come to think of it. Patience was *not* a virtue he possessed. Still, something inside him held out hope. Told him to continue to pretend to read, even though he'd been staring at the same page of the book he'd opened for what felt like hours.

And then—finally—just as he was giving up hope, just as he was about to toss the bloody book aside and march up to his bedchamber, the door burst open, and Clare rushed inside. She was breathless and beautiful, her golden hair slightly mussed from her hasty movements. Her long limbs all fluid and graceful as she flew into the room like a goddess.

Relief. That's what hit him first. Pure, undeniable relief.

"There you are," he said before he could stop himself. Damn it.

Her lips quirked. "I thought you'd be gone by now," she said rather breathlessly.

Ah, there was that refreshing candor again. Most of the women in his acquaintance wrapped their words in careful implication, laced with coy glances and false innocence.

Clare Handleton didn't waste time with such nonsense.

Honesty deserved honesty in return.

"I was just about to leave," he admitted. "I thought you weren't coming."

"My mother was up later than expected," she said, rolling her eyes and smoothing down her flaxen hair. "Reading, no doubt."

"Really?" he drawled. "What does she like to read?"

A sharp laugh escaped Clare. "Treatises on how to handle scandal-ridden daughters, no doubt."

Ash couldn't help his smile. She was funny, Lady Clare.

Funny, self-deprecating, and sharp. All things he admired. He narrowed his eyes at her. Tonight, she wore a bright-blue gown instead of a chemise. A real pity.

"Why weren't you at dinner?" he asked before realizing he should have been more subtle about it.

Clare lifted a brow. "Didn't Meredith tell you?"

"She said you had a megrim."

"And?" A hint of amusement played at the edges of her full lips. "You doubted her?"

"Let's just say," he said as he moved to the sideboard, "you don't strike me as a woman who suffers from megrims."

He poured two fingers of brandy into a glass. He briefly considered pouring two glasses, but something told him she should be the one to decide if he drank tonight.

So he turned, extending the drink toward her. "Ladies first."

She took it without hesitation, lifted it to her lips, and downed a hefty portion without so much as a blink.

Not even a cough.

He chuckled, watching her. "The lady can obviously hold her liquor."

Clare handed the glass back to him, her fingers warm against his. "Are you surprised?"

"Not in the least." He lifted the glass to his lips but didn't drink. Instead, he tilted his head. "Do you have this at home?"

She gave him a knowing look. "Are you asking if I drink this every night?"

Astute. *Very astute.*

"Yes, that's what I'm asking." More honesty.

"Nearly every night." She said it so matter-of-factly, as if it wasn't something most women would never dare to admit. "Just enough to calm my nerves."

He had expected her to dodge the question, to make a joke, to evade. Instead, she told him the truth again.

And he would be a hypocrite if he faulted her for it.

"I drink nearly every night too," he said, taking a sip and handing the glass back to her.

She studied him. "For your nerves?" A slow smile played around her lips, teasing and clever.

"For the hell of it."

That made her laugh. And damn if that sound didn't do something to him. It was as if, in this room, they had made a silent pact—no lies, no games, only honesty.

It felt so damn good.

But then something shifted. Clare went quiet, running her fingertip along the rim of the glass, eyes focused on the amber liquid inside. She took a sip and handed him the glass. He took one too.

"Would you kiss me?" she asked suddenly.

Ash nearly choked. He laughed, shaking his head. "No."

A beat of silence. Then, with an edge of something unreadable, she asked, "Why not?"

He slapped his chest, still trying to right the choking. "Isn't it obvious?"

She narrowed her eyes at him. "Because I'm not pretty enough for you?"

That nearly made him spit out his brandy.

"What?" he barked, incredulous. "Christ, no."

She just watched him, waiting, blinking at him with those unfathomable dark eyes of hers. Intelligent, watchful eyes that seemed to take in everything all at once.

He exhaled, forcing himself to focus. "Frankly, I don't want you to think I'm trying to take advantage of you."

She tilted her head slightly, considering. "What if I have a quite specific and quite good *reason* to ask you to kiss me?"

Ash handed the glass back to her, then he crossed his arms, eyeing her warily. "This ought to be good."

Clare lifted her chin and gave her head a little shake.

"Marsden was the first and only man who has ever kissed me."

A muscle in Ash's jaw clenched. *Marsden was a horse's ass.*

"I don't want him to be the last," she continued. "I need to know if he was even any good."

Ash bit his lip. Oh, damn. *Careful, Trentham.*

"I can tell you now," he said slowly, allowing the barest hint of amusement to play about his lips, "knowing Marsden, he's a rubbish kisser."

"I don't doubt it." She took another small sip from the glass, her voice quieter now, more thoughtful. "But can you not take pity on me?" She blinked at him, her black eyelashes impossibly long, her pink lips ridiculously tempting.

Ash's stomach tightened.

"I'd like a kiss that will wipe the memory of his from my mind forever." She paused, then added, "And I'm convinced *you're* the man to do it."

Ash stilled. He had never been one to hesitate when a beautiful woman asked him for a kiss. He had stolen them in dark corridors, in moonlit gardens, in empty salons.

But this wasn't just any woman.

This was Clare Handleton.

And something told him—something deep in his bones— that if he kissed her, there would be no forgetting it. Not for her. Not for him.

So he did the one thing he never did.

He hesitated.

CHAPTER FIVE

Clare watched Ashford Drake carefully from beneath her lashes, her pulse thrumming in her ears. She was playing with fire, and she knew it. But she didn't give a damn.

When would an opportunity like this ever present itself again?

For years, she had been hidden away in her late father's country house, a ghost of her former self. The *ton* gossiped about her unmercifully while she remained locked behind gilded bars. Her father had died when she was a girl, so at least he hadn't lived to witness his only child's disgrace. And her mother saw to it that she never forgot it. Few outings. No social calls. Just one pitying trip to London each year for shopping, where she was reminded—always reminded—that she no longer belonged.

But *this*—this was freedom.

Meredith's country house party was the one event in all these years that her mother had begrudgingly allowed her to attend, and Clare wasn't about to squander the only real chance she had.

Because she had told Ash the truth.

She wanted this.

She wanted to erase the memory of the Earl of Marsden's kisses from her mind forever.

That bastard had ruined her. And she had walked willingly into his trap, mistaking charm for affection, mistaking her own desperation for love. She had no one to blame but herself—and she knew it. She had long since made peace with her actions, had taken responsibility for her choices, but it didn't erase the regret.

Regret that she would never get to kiss a man again, let alone find love, marry, give birth to children. Of course, Marsden had suffered much less than she had. He'd left town briefly, gone to the Continent. Stayed away for about six whole months. What a sacrifice!

Then he'd returned to pick up right where he'd left off. He courted another young woman, married her, and proceeded to have half a dozen children. Of course, to this day, he was still known for his indiscretions and his poor wife was pitied behind closed doors, but the man himself had paid no real penance. It was unfair at best, nearly criminal at worse.

And the thing Clare most detested was that the one memory she had of making love was with a selfish, careless bastard who had taught her nothing and taken everything.

She refused to accept that. She wanted a new fate.

She wanted a new kiss. A *real* kiss. A good one, administered by a man who knew precisely what he was about. And this time, it would be from a man worthy of kissing.

Trentham scratched the back of his neck, his brow furrowed. "I'm not certain—"

"Please don't tell me you're not certain that it's a good idea," she interrupted, quite businesslike. "Of course, it's not a good idea. But neither is meeting down here in the middle of the night and drinking brandy we have not been offered." She cocked her head, a teasing smile playing at her lips. "Besides, I didn't think you were one for valuing good ideas at all times. Was I mistaken?"

Ash's eyes flared slightly at that, and she knew she had struck a nerve.

Because he loved being the *ton*'s most scandalous lord. He reveled in it.

He was the man who flouted convention, the man who publicly swore off marriage just to spite his dead father. He was reckless, unpredictable, and wholly unconcerned with what anyone thought.

So why was he hesitating now?

"You want me to kiss you?" he asked, his voice low, his gaze assessing. There was something in his expression she recognized.

Interest.

Dare she hope…lust?

"Yes," she said simply, nodding. She needed to treat this with no emotion whatsoever. Emotion would only scare off a man like Ash. She didn't want to force him into marriage. On the contrary, she only wanted one simple kiss.

His lips twitched. "And what if it doesn't meet your standards?"

Her brows shot up. "You and I both know you're far too confident to allow that to happen."

That made him laugh, slow and rich, and damn him, but he was even more handsome when he smiled. The dark hair. The gray eyes. The mouth that looked like it was made for sin. Hell, his profile alone made her knees weak.

"Flattering me now?" he mused.

She shrugged one shoulder. *Hmm.* So he was clever enough to see through that? "If it will get me what I want."

He bit his lip. A sign of hesitation?

She decided to push.

"Just one kiss," she murmured. "That's all I ask."

He sighed, rubbing a hand over his jaw. "You're my sister's closest friend."

She arched a brow. "What does that have to do with anything?"

He put his hands on his hips, exhaled, then laughed, staring down at the rug. "Nothing, I suppose. I just had to say it out loud."

She splayed her free hand wide, still committed to convincing him. "I'm not expecting you to ask me to dance in a ballroom full of people. I'm only asking you to kiss me once, here, where only the two of us will know." She gave him a coy smile. "If it helps, I'm sure Meredith would approve."

That made him pause. His head lifted, and he narrowed his gaze at her. "Would she?"

"Oh, certainly." She gave an exaggerated shrug. "She already knows what a rubbish kisser Marsden was. I told her."

Ash barked a laugh, rubbing the back of his neck. "I'm actually thinking about doing this," he breathed.

"Good," she blurted as a thrill shot through her.

Then he moved.

A single step brought him closer, and before she could react, he plucked the snifter from her hand, setting it aside on the desk.

Her breath hitched.

Then—slowly, deliberately—he curled his hands beneath her elbows, his touch firm but gentle.

Her heart thundered.

He was so close now. Close enough that she could feel the heat radiating from his body, close enough that she could smell the faint trace of brandy on his breath.

He leaned down, his voice a husky whisper against her ear.

"Do you want me to kiss you," he murmured, "or do *you* want to kiss *me*?"

Clare's hands shook. She hadn't expected to be this successful quite so quickly. She met his gaze, her pulse fluttering like a trapped bird. "Is there a difference?" she asked, her voice trembling slightly.

"Oh, yes," he said, his lips curving into a roughish grin. "Quite a large one."

She swallowed. "Which one will be more pleasurable?"

The smile that crossed his face was *devastating*. "That depends."

He reached up, brushing a loose strand of hair from her temple, his fingers grazing her skin. She shuddered.

"Kiss me," she breathed.

And before she could even draw another breath, he had gathered her hair in one hand, tugging her head back—not painfully, but firmly—and then his mouth was on hers.

And *dear God, he could kiss.*

The first brush of his lips was slow, testing, coaxing—but then he deepened it, tilting her head back farther as he licked into her mouth, hot and sure and utterly consuming.

Her hands fisted in the fabric of his waistcoat, desperate for purchase as he took control. As he ruined her for any other kiss that might follow.

When his lips left hers, she barely had time to catch her breath before she felt the warm press of his mouth against her neck.

Her fingers dug into his shoulders. "Ash—"

He made a sound deep in his throat, half growl, half something else, as his lips brushed the delicate skin just beneath her jaw.

A shiver ran down her spine.

His hand slid to her waist, his fingers spreading over her hip, gripping her just enough to make her burn.

And oh God, she wanted more.

When he finally pulled away, she was breathless.

"Well?" he murmured, his forehead resting against hers, his breathing slightly labored. "Did that erase Marsden's kiss from your memory?"

She grinned, wicked and triumphant. "What kiss with Marsden?"

Then, before he could respond, she gathered her skirts and turned toward the door. "Thank you," she said.

"Wait," he called, frowning.

She paused, her hand on the latch, glancing back. "What?"

Ash hesitated, looking as if he didn't quite know what he was about to say.

Then, finally—quietly—he asked, "Why me?"

Clare blinked.

He swallowed, his voice softer now. "Why did you ask *me* to kiss you?"

A long sigh left her lips, her shoulders rising and falling. Then she let out a small laugh, shaking her head. "I suppose now would be the time to confess that I've been infatuated with you for absolute ages." She winked. "Thank you for making my dreams come true."

Then she was gone.

AND ASH, still standing there, could only stare after her, wondering what the hell had just happened.

CHAPTER SIX

The gardens at Southbury Hall were in full autumnal bloom, the air thick with the scent of orange roses and black-eyed rudbeckia as Clare, Meredith, and Gemma strolled through the winding paths, wicker baskets in hand, gathering flowers for the evening's centerpiece arrangements. There was to be a ball tonight, and all the house party guests would be in attendance.

The afternoon sun cast a golden glow over everything, but their conversation was far from idyllic.

"It's a lost cause trying to get Lord Trentham to pick a wife," Gemma Banks said, carefully selecting a pale-yellow daisy. Gemma was several years younger than the other two ladies, but they both adored her.

Gemma's small brown terrier, Oliver, ran around his mistress's heels, jumping at the butterflies that circled in the air.

Meredith sighed, rubbing her temple and placing a gloved hand atop her burgeoning belly. "How can you tell?"

"He ignores the lot of them—the debutantes you so carefully picked out," Gemma replied with a sympathetic smile. Gemma herself had recently married the Duke of Grovemont. After a contentious start to their marriage, she and Lucian were now madly in love, though they'd been embroiled in a scandal that Clare had helped them navigate.

"And I spent *so much* time picking them," Meredith groaned.

Clare smirked, snipping a rose from the bush. "Hearing all of this makes me quite glad I don't have to deal with any of it."

Gemma suddenly stilled, her expression turning thoughtful as she reached out and touched Clare's arm. "Oh, dear. I'm sorry to have brought it up in front of you. It was thoughtless of me."

Clare waved her off with an easy shrug. "Oh, don't worry. I'm long since past it."

Gemma bit her lip, hesitating before speaking again. "May I ask you a question, Lady Clare?"

"Of course, dear. And how many times have I told you that you may simply call me Clare?"

Gemma smiled and nodded. "You helped Lucian and me when we needed you. You fixed our scandal. You clearly know how. I've always wondered...why have you never employed those same skills to restore your own reputation?"

Clare went very still, her gloved fingers tightening around the stem of her rose.

For a moment, she only glanced between Gemma and Meredith, feeling the weight of their expectant stares. No one had ever asked her this before. Though it stood to reason they would wonder. After all, Clare was known among certain people in the *ton* for being the lady to go to when a scandal had reared its ugly, unwanted head. She'd had plenty of experience with the subject, after all. And she knew precisely how to clean things up. And there was a very good reason she'd never employed her skills to fix her own situation.

Clare finally sighed. "The truth is, I'd rather deal with my controlling mother than a controlling husband."

"Really?" Meredith asked, frowning. "I never knew you felt that way, Clare."

"Yes, well." Clare gave a dry smile. "There's a certain amount of freedom I enjoy—slipping away from Mama from time to time. She falls asleep so often now that she's getting older." She let out a short laugh, though there was no real humor in it. "If I had restored my own reputation, I'd be obliged to marry, and I'm not interested in marriage in the least."

"I suppose I understand why you'd rather not marry," Gemma said softly. "But Lucian is *such* a dear." Her eyes grew soft and misty as she thought of her beloved husband.

"And I cannot imagine my life without my Griffin," Meredith added with an equally wistful smile.

Clare rolled her eyes and waved a hand in the air. "I know. I know. You're both quite in *love*, but it's not like that for most ladies of the *ton*. And I have no intention of making myself another grim statistic. With or without my scandalous past."

Meredith sighed, shaking her head. "Well, in that case, let's focus on other people's love lives. Ash may be resisting my efforts, but at least Cecily and Lord Albion seem to be enjoying each other's company."

"Oh, yes," Gemma said, nodding as she reached down to scoop Oliver into her arms. "Cecily is quite enamored with Lord Albion. Just this morning, she said she cannot thank you enough for inviting him here."

Cecily was Gemma's closest friend and still unmarried. They were all hoping for a betrothal by the end of the house party.

"At least someone is benefitting from my matchmaking efforts," Meredith replied with a laugh, just before a determined look brightened her eye. "But we're having a dance tonight, and I fully intend to threaten my elusive brother with bodily harm if he doesn't choose a lady to dance with."

Clare arched a brow. "Do you really think that will work? I honestly cannot picture Trentham asking anyone to dance. He isn't exactly the dancing sort." The *kissing* sort? Yes. Dancing? No.

Meredith scowled. "Well, he'd better become the dancing sort…and quickly. If not, I may just trip him into someone's arms."

Gemma giggled. Clare only sighed, shaking her head.

Tonight was going to be interesting indeed.

CHAPTER SEVEN

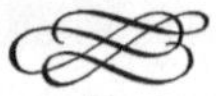

The massive chandeliers hanging from the ceiling cast a golden glow over Southbury's ballroom, illuminating the swirling silks and satins of some of London's finest as they glided across the polished floor. The scent of beeswax, expensive perfume, and the sharp tang of champagne filled the air, mingling with the soft strains of the orchestra.

Ash exhaled slowly, adjusting the cuffs of his pristine ivory shirt beneath the midnight-blue velvet of his overcoat. His waistcoat, a shade lighter, was embroidered with silver thread, subtle but decadent, paired with an immaculate snowy-white cravat fastened by a sapphire pin. He looked every inch the marquess his sister so desperately wished he would behave like.

Unfortunately for Meredith, tonight was not going to be one of those nights.

She had threatened him—actually threatened him—if he didn't choose a lady to dance with, she would trot one over and foist her upon him.

The problem was every eligible debutante she had hand-selected for his consideration and invited to this blasted house party had turned out to be a complete bore.

Simpering, shallow, utterly predictable.

They echoed back his own thoughts as if they had none of their own, their conversation limited to their latest gowns, the next ball, and which gentleman had the most agreeable prospects. Most annoying, however, was their tendency to stare at him as if he were a prized pig. He found few things as unattractive as desperation, and he could smell the desperation on every single one of the ladies Meredith had invited.

Was this truly the best selection Meredith could find?

If so, he would remain single indefinitely, thank you very much.

"What about Lady Julia? She's sweet," Meredith had pleaded earlier, right before the threatening had commenced.

"Sweet? Sweet is a word reserved for pastries and children. I'm not looking for sweet."

Far from it, if he was looking for anyone, she would be quite the opposite. Someone intriguing, daring, unforgettable. Someone like…Clare.

After their kiss last night, he'd been unable to *stop* thinking about her, actually.

His sister might not believe it, but he *did* intend to ask a lady to dance tonight.

One Lady Clare Handleton.

And the devil take the consequences.

Oh, it would cause talk. He could practically hear the whispers already. Lady Clare—*Scandalton*—had likely not been asked to dance since her debut year. And yet, here he was, prepared to make a spectacle of the entire evening.

He had every intention of setting the *ton*'s tongues wagging tonight. And he could not recall the last time he'd been looking forward to something so much.

He'd made the decision last night. There had been something about the way Clare had said the words so casually. *"I'm not expecting you to ask me to dance in a ballroom full of people. I'm only asking you to kiss me once, here, where only the two of us will know."* Those words were burned into his mind. He couldn't forget them. Clare had been relegated to the shadows for so long that she no longer thought herself worthy of regard. She assumed no decent man would ever be so bold as to ask her to dance. And Ash intended to do something about it. Immediately.

Of course, their kiss had left a lasting impression on him too, one he didn't dare dwell upon for long lest his breeches become too tight. Not quite a decent state of affairs for a ballroom in his sister's house. But regardless of his indecent thoughts about Lady Clare, he intended to ask her to dance. He could only *hope* she would accept the invitation.

His gaze scanned the room until—*there.*

Across the ballroom, near a cluster of dowagers and wallflowers, stood Clare.

She was dressed in a gown the color of flames at sunset, rich and deep, catching the candlelight in molten waves as she shifted. The cut of the gown hugged her curves, the daring dip of the neckline offset by the elegant sweep of her shoulders. Her golden hair was pinned in a deceptively careless chignon, a few errant curls trailing down the nape of her neck in a way that made his fingers twitch with the sudden, overwhelming urge to touch them.

She took his breath away.

Ash ignored the longing stares of the debutantes, including Lady Julia, and the sharp, assessing gaze of his sister, and strode across the ballroom directly toward Clare.

Her back was to him as she spoke to Gemma, seemingly unaware of the ripple of awareness sweeping across the room. The moment he stopped behind her, the conversation halted.

She turned, her expression unreadable—until her dark eyes met his.

A flicker of surprise. Suspicion. Amusement.

And then wariness.

"Lady Clare," Ash said smoothly, bowing slightly. "Would you do me the honor of this dance?"

Silence.

Absolute, deafening silence.

Clare blinked, glancing around as if expecting someone to correct him.

"Me?" She pointed at her middle.

He arched a brow. "I see no other Lady Clare in attendance."

She hesitated. Just for a moment. Then—slowly, deliberately—she placed her gloved hand in his.

"Yes," she said simply.

The orchestra struck the first notes of a waltz.

Perfect timing.

Ash curled his fingers around hers, relishing the way she fit so neatly against him as he led her onto the dance floor.

The moment their hands met, the room shifted.

Everyone was watching.

Clare *felt* it—he could see it in the way her shoulders tensed, the way her gaze darted briefly to the gathered onlookers.

Let them watch.

"Strange," Ash mused, his voice low as he guided her effortlessly through the first turn. "I don't believe I've ever seen you look nervous before."

Her spine straightened instantly. "I am not nervous."

He bit back a smile. There was her spirit again. "Good. I'd hate to think I was intimidating you."

She scoffed. "You? Never."

This time, he did smile.

They moved in perfect synchrony, as if they had danced together a hundred times before. As he spun around, he caught his sister's gaze on the sidelines and gave her a very smug smile. Meredith's mouth was gaping open. He blinked at her innocently.

"Thank you for dancing with me," he said to Clare.

Her grip tightened on his shoulder. "Thank you for asking. I do hope you realize how much gossip we're causing."

"Better to be the cause of gossip than the gossiper," he said, grinning down at her.

Clare smiled and shook her head. "I don't believe I've ever met anyone with less regard for what others think of them." She paused for a beat. "Besides myself, that is."

Ash threw back his head and laughed. "Then we are clearly a well-matched pair."

"Don't look now, but Lady Julia Fairbanks's glare may burn a hole in your coat."

Ash sighed. "Ah, that is the second time Lady Julia's name has been mentioned to me today, and I can't say I care any more now than I did the first time I heard it."

"She's considered the catch of the Season," Clare informed him.

"Good for her." Ash's smile was droll.

Clare slapped his shoulder and gave him a fake-stern stare. "Your sister went to great lengths to bring these ladies here. The least you could do is pretend to be interested."

"Never." His stare penetrated her. "When I am truly interested, a lady knows it."

Clare glanced away. Her throat worked as she swallowed.

"So," he murmured, bending slightly to whisper in her ear, "am I to expect you in the study again tonight?"

She lifted her chin, lips curving up. "I did not think we had an appointment, my lord."

His grip on her waist tightened ever so slightly. Oh, she was an intriguing one, to be sure. "We don't. Yet. I'm asking you now."

Her eyes sparkled with amusement…and curiosity. "Don't you think that dangerous?"

"Oh, I know it's dangerous. But I was under the distinct impression that you and I aren't dissuaded by danger."

She gave him a reluctant smile. "I do not like to tempt fate."

He allowed a hint of skepticism to touch his lips. "Don't you?"

Clare's observant eyes darted about the enormous room. "We're already causing gossip. We're certain to be watched more closely after this."

Ash blew out a frustrated breath. He lowered his voice to a sultry whisper. "So that's it? One kiss? That's all you wanted from me?"

One of her elegant brows shot up. "Oh, now. I *never* said that."

CHAPTER EIGHT

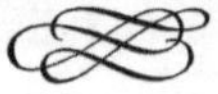

Ashford Drake had never been a man easily distracted. He had spent years cultivating an air of nonchalance, of indifference to everything and everyone who didn't serve a direct purpose in his life. And until quite recently—this week, in fact—that had worked splendidly.

Now, however, he was distracted as hell.

And it was entirely Clare Handleton's fault.

He was supposed to be enjoying this bloody house party, mingling with the eligible debutantes his sister had so helpfully assembled for him, and spending time with some of his closest friends. But instead, he sat at breakfast ignoring Lady Penelope's insipid remarks about the weather, half-listening to Lord Hastwell drone on about some estate in Derbyshire, and barely pretending to care about the details of the croquet match the ladies were organizing for the afternoon.

His mind was consumed with *her*.

With her sharp little smirk, the way her breath had caught when he touched her, the feel of her mouth against his.

And worst of all—what she had said right before she left him after that kiss.

"I suppose now would be the time to confess that I've been infatuated with you for absolute ages."

Those were the words he couldn't erase from his memory. *Didn't want to erase.*

Damn her.

She hadn't appeared in the study last night either. He'd waited around like a foolish lad with a schoolboy's fancy. He'd tried to read the same blasted uninteresting book again, paced in front of the fireplace for what felt like hours. He'd even downed nearly three glasses of brandy. But she hadn't arrived.

By the time he returned to his room and fell backwards onto his bed in a frustrated heap last night, he supposed it was for the best. After all, it wasn't as if they could have a *future* together. Despite his sister's insistence on his taking a wife, he was a confirmed bachelor, and Lady Clare was a ruined woman. A match between them, or even a friendship between them, was unthinkable. It was only prudent to cut things off after one kiss.

But when he awoke this morning, the memory of Clare dancing in his arms last night, was the first thought in his head, and he hadn't been able to think of much else since. That and the impudent comment she'd made at the end of their dance. He couldn't get any of it out of his mind. By the time the midday sun streamed through the tall, mullioned windows of Southbury Hall, Ash was thoroughly done with pretending to be interested in anything else.

It was true. He'd never been so distracted, and there was only one thing he could think to do about it. He had to learn more about what she'd said.

And then, as if summoned by sheer will, he saw her.

She was alone, walking down the corridor toward the

west wing, seemingly unaware of the havoc she had wrought upon his thoughts. Her hair gleamed in the soft light, her expression unreadable, her figure far too tempting in that pale-green day dress.

He acted without thinking.

Lifting a hand, he caught her attention with a subtle motion, inclining his head toward an open doorway.

Her brows lifted slightly, but after the barest hesitation, and a quick glance about, she slipped inside.

Ash followed, shutting the door behind him.

The drawing room was quiet, the heavy drapes drawn just enough to soften the afternoon light. The scent of polished wood and fresh flowers hung in the air, but Ash barely registered it.

All he could sense was her.

Clare folded her arms across her chest, regarding him with that same damned knowing half-smile that had been driving him mad for days. "Well, this is intriguing," she said lightly. "Is this how you lure women into empty rooms, my lord?"

"Only the ones who kiss me senseless and then disappear into the night," he shot back.

Her lips twitched, but she held his gaze steadily. "I don't recall you putting up much of a fight."

"I was too busy trying to keep my wits about me," he admitted, stepping closer. "Not that it worked."

Something flickered in her expression—something pleased. "Also, I seem to recall that *you* kissed *me*," she added.

She liked knowing she had unsettled him. He could tell.

He exhaled sharply. "What exactly did you mean, Clare?"

Her brows furrowed. "About what?"

"Don't play coy." His voice dropped slightly. "When you said you'd been infatuated with me forever—what exactly did you mean?"

Her lips parted slightly, as if surprised by his insistence. Then, after a beat, she lifted her chin and said, "Just what I said."

Ash's stomach tightened.

He had been prepared for teasing, for deflection, for one of her sharp little quips.

But not for honesty. Not for the simple, matter-of-fact way she said it.

And that? That did something to him.

A muscle worked in his jaw. "A man cannot erase such a thing from his memory."

Clare tilted her head slightly, studying him. Then she smiled. A slow, knowing smile. "Then we are even because I don't think I can erase such a kiss from my memory either."

Ash stilled. Heat unfurled low in his stomach, something dangerous and utterly consuming taking root.

Hell.

She wasn't playing any longer.

Neither was he.

He took another step forward, closing the space between them. Slowly. Deliberately. Watching the way her breath hitched as he moved closer.

"Then," he murmured, voice husky with intent, "what do you propose we do about it?"

CHAPTER NINE

Clare sat perched on the edge of a velvet chaise, pretending to listen as Meredith prattled on about her brother's utter failure to show any real interest in the carefully selected young ladies assembled under this roof.

Across the room, Meredith's lady's maid, Martha, fastened the last delicate pearl at the nape of the duchess's neck. Meredith looked stunning, as always, in an emerald silk gown that set off her dark hair and clear gray eyes—eyes that looked like her brother's, eyes that were currently narrowed in frustration.

"Honestly," Meredith huffed, studying herself in the looking glass, "it would be just like Ash to ruin this."

Clare blinked, dragging her thoughts—or attempting to—back to the present. "Ruin what, exactly?"

"This opportunity," Meredith said, turning to face her, arms crossed. "Do you have any idea how carefully I selected these ladies? Each of them is perfectly suitable. Refined, accomplished, attractive, well-bred. Any one of them would make an excellent match, and yet my dear brother,"—she threw her hands in the air—"has shown interest in precisely none of them."

Clare shifted in her seat, heart still pounding far too hard from what had transpired earlier.

What shall we do about it?

The words had followed her out of that drawing room, chased her all the way back to her chambers, and had not left her alone since.

Even now, she could feel the sensation of Ash's breath against her skin, the heat in his gaze, the way he had looked at her as if she were the only thing in the world worth looking at.

She swallowed hard, fingers digging into the fabric of her skirts.

"I mean, really," Meredith went on, oblivious to her friend's inner turmoil, "he couldn't have made this easier for me? No flirtations, no dances that linger just a bit too long? I swear, he's ignoring them all on purpose. And though it was lovely of him to ask *you* to dance, I can't help but think he did it just to provoke me."

Clare frowned. "What do you mean?"

"I threatened him to pick someone, and he picked my dearest friend? Utterly aggravating." Meredith shook her head.

"I would take offense at that, if I hadn't just told you recently how uninterested I am in marriage," Clare replied with a laugh.

She didn't blame Meredith for the sentiment. After all, she would have no social life whatsoever if it weren't for Meredith. Not to mention the fact that even after all these years, Clare had never told her best friend that she harbored a secret attraction to her older brother. Given her scandal, it would hardly be appropriate for Ash to court her, and Clare had never wanted to put Meredith in an awkward position.

Meredith turned in her seat to face her friend. "Oh, Clare, darling, I meant no offense, of course. I only mean that he has his *pick* of debutantes, and yet he spends his time with you and me and Gemma, all of whom he can see any time he likes. Meanwhile, he's squandering his chance with the debutantes. Lady Julia Fairbanks is considered the *diamond* of the Season, for heaven's sake."

Clare shuddered, remembering how Lady Julia had given her a particularly condemning glare last night after she'd finished her dance with Ash. If looks could kill, Clare would have dropped dead on the spot. It was obvious Lady Julia had her sights set on him.

Clare forced herself to respond, though her voice felt far away. "Perhaps none of the debutantes are to his liking."

Meredith scoffed. "Nonsense. I cast a wide net. There's a type for everyone. Some men prefer delicate and demure, others clever and confident, others bold and vivacious—he has options."

Clare swallowed against the sudden heat that coiled low in her belly. *Bold and vivacious.*

Hadn't Ash told her that she wasn't the sort of woman to suffer from megrims? That she was different? That she didn't strike him as a woman who needed to be handled gently?

He was right.

Her breath hitched.

Meredith let out another exasperated sigh, adjusting the heavy diamond bracelet on her wrist. "I don't suppose you have any insight into this mystery?"

Clare blinked. "What?"

"My brother." Meredith turned to look at her. "If none of these ladies are catching his eye, who *do* you think he should pick?"

Clare's mouth went dry.

Ash *pinning her against the desk* in the study, his fingers clutching her elbows.

Ash breathing against her ear, whispering, *Do you want me to kiss you, or do you want to kiss me?*

Ash's lips on hers, burning away every trace of the past, every bitter memory of Marsden, replacing them with something hot and consuming and utterly unforgettable.

Clare shook her head. This was madness. She was *not* going to have an affair with Ashford Drake. That was unacceptable. Unbelievable. Untenable. No. In addition to being wrong, it could cause her to ruin her carefully laid plans. She was so close now. Another scandal would ruin everything. And of all the men to court scandal with, Ash was the most egregious. It would not only risk her friendship with Meredith, it would also risk Clare's very existence.

But even knowing all of that, she couldn't help the fact that her pulse raced at the memory of Ash's touch. She already knew…if he tried to kiss her again, she would participate. Eagerly. The room still felt stiflingly warm.

Meredith raised a brow. "Clare?"

Clare forced a slow inhale, praying her voice wouldn't betray her. Something sharp and sinful twisted inside her as she met her friend's gaze, the words slipping from her lips before she could stop them. "I wouldn't worry about Ash," she murmured, her voice just a little too smooth. "Something tells me your brother knows *precisely* what he's doing."

Meredith groaned, rubbing a hand atop her belly. "Well, I wish he would get on with it then."

Clare only just managed to hold back her smile.

CHAPTER TEN

Ash had never been a man to obsess over a woman. He had spent years cultivating a reputation as the devil-may-care rakehell, the man who enjoyed a flirtation, a brief indulgence, a short-lived affair before moving on.

It wasn't that he was incapable of attachment—he just never saw the point. Plus, there was the added delight that remaining a bachelor indefinitely would ensure that his bastard of a father—God rest the horrid man's soul—would never have another heir.

Women were lovely, of course. Amusing, charming, sometimes even interesting. But never more than temporary distractions. And even though he'd lost a bet with Southbury last year and promised to look for a wife as a result, Meredith and Griffin had to be reasonable. Some men just weren't meant to marry…and Ash was clearly one of them.

Yet here he was *burning* for Clare Handleton.

And it was utterly unlike him.

He had kissed her once. Only once.

It should not have been enough to unsettle him. It should

not have been enough to consume him. And yet he couldn't stop thinking about her. It was a damned nuisance, really.

He had spent the entire day restless and on edge, pacing the grounds, attempting conversation, drinking more than was necessary just to numb the ache of wanting her.

It hadn't worked.

Everything about her haunted him—the taste of her, the sound of her breath catching as he kissed her, the way she had whispered, "Kiss me," like a plea and a challenge all at once.

And that *damned confession.*

"I've been infatuated with you for absolute ages."

Hell.

Every time he closed his eyes, he saw her standing in that study, all teasing smirks and knowing glances, as if she hadn't completely undone him.

And the worst part? He knew—*knew*—he couldn't cross a certain line with her.

She wasn't like the other women who drifted in and out of his life, leaving behind only a pleasant memory and a vague sense of amusement.

Clare was different.

She had been branded by scandal. She had been cast aside, left with nothing but her defiance and that wicked, sharp smile. He knew if he took things too far, if he went any further than kissing, *she* would bear the brunt of the consequences—not him.

But none of that changed the fact that he wanted her.

Badly.

Good God. Why couldn't he just forget it? Forget that kiss? Forget her? But he already suspected that he knew why. She'd been the one to put an end to things. She'd been the one to walk away. In the past, he'd always been the one to end things with any lady, no matter how insignificant their dalliance. He wasn't proud of the fact that he couldn't resist a challenge. But it was true. He needed one more kiss. One more kiss just to prove to himself that she was merely a woman like any other. Then he would put her out of his mind forever.

But he had to move quickly. There was only one night left of the house party.

He couldn't leave without seeing her again. To that end, he'd sent his *very* discreet valet with a note to her room, asking her to meet him tonight in the study one last time.

And when the house finally settled into silence, when the guests had all retired to their bedchambers, he took another chance. He made his way down to Southbury's study.

And he waited.

Of course, he wasn't even certain she would come. No doubt she was still hesitant to risk her reputation further. Perhaps she had decided after all that one kiss *was* all she wanted from him.

Perhaps she had gone to bed, completely unbothered, while he sat here like a fool, hard and aching and utterly wrecked with wanting her.

He scrubbed a hand through his hair. The clock on the mantel ticked. He didn't even pretend to read the bloody book this time. He just sat there, staring into the fireplace, hoping with every part of himself that she was as interested in one last stolen moment with him as he was with her.

And then—*finally*—he heard the soft creak of the door.

He stood and turned just as Clare stepped inside the room.

And the moment she saw him, she sucked in her breath.

It was barely audible, just the faintest intake of air—but it told him *everything*.

She was pleased to see him.

Good.

Because he was half-mad with wanting her.

Ash tilted his head, watching as she shut the door behind her, pressing her hands to the door behind her back.

"This is our last night," he murmured.

Clare held his gaze, her expression unreadable—but he saw the faint flush that crept up her throat, saw the way her fingers twitched at her sides.

"So it would seem," she murmured back.

Ash studied her, his fingers clutching the back of the chair he stood behind, resisting the urge to cross the room and touch her.

"'Would seem?'" he repeated, his voice low. "That's not quite definitive."

Clare's lips curled slightly, as if she had expected him to latch onto that. She stepped forward, but not too close—just enough to tease him with her presence, with the maddening scent of her perfume. Like orchids. Perfect for her. Unique and compelling. "All good things must come to an end," she said lightly.

That shouldn't have stung. But it did.

He pushed the chair aside and stalked toward her, resisting the urge at the last minute to grab her hand. Instead, he watched her face. "Where will you go after tomorrow?"

"I'm going back to London," she said. "Meredith invited me to stay with her for the autumn Season, and Mama has agreed."

Ash swore under his breath. "That's going to be an unholy temptation for me." He had his own town house in London, but he was often at Southbury's house, spending time with his sister and his closest friend.

Clare let out a small laugh, the sound wicked and knowing. "I expect you'll find a way to manage."

Doubtful.

Highly doubtful.

Ash had spent the last twenty-four hours doing a rubbish job of managing himself, and that had been with the entire house party as a buffer.

Now, she was going to be in his sister's home? Within reach? A temptation laid before him nearly daily?

God help him.

"I'm not entirely sure why I came here tonight," she announced. "You know as well as I do that there can be nothing else between you and me." She said the words far too casually, as if they weren't a decision so much as a decree. Then Clare turned back toward the door, pausing just as she reached for the handle. She glanced at him over her shoulder, her golden hair gleaming in the candlelight.

She was waiting for something.

For him to stop her?

For him to say something reckless and irreversible?

He did nothing.

Because he knew that if he touched her now, he wouldn't be able to stop.

So he let her go.

But as the door clicked shut behind her, one thing became unbearably clear.

Things were *not* over between him and Clare Handleton.

Not at all.

CHAPTER ELEVEN

Clare had nearly made it back to her room when a sound across the corridor made her pause. She turned sharply, pulse hammering, just in time to see the shadows shift near the window.

"Who's there?" she demanded, heart lodged somewhere between her ribs and her throat.

The curtains stirred, and Lady Julia Fairbanks stepped out.

Clare let out a breath, pressing a hand to her chest. "Good Lord, Lady Julia, I nearly died of fright."

"Did you?" Julia's voice was honeyed poison, smooth but laced with something sharper underneath.

Clare's spine stiffened. If she'd merely suspected the debutante was up to no good before, she was certain of it now.

Julia moved toward her with a deliberate grace, the hem of her dressing gown skimming the floor. She stopped just in front of Clare, making no attempt to disguise the slow, calculating way her gaze raked her from head to toe. The disdain on her face was almost impressive in its effort.

Clare lifted her chin, her expression settling into a perfectly neutral mask. She'd long grown used to the judgment of those who considered themselves superior. It was practically a sport among the well-bred—eyeing her like a bit of spoiled fruit. Honestly, it was getting boring.

"I was just going to bed," she said evenly, fingers curling around the door handle. "Goodnight."

"Wait." The order was clipped, practiced. No doubt Julia was used to getting what she wanted.

Clare shut her eyes for a moment before turning, mustering every last scrap of patience she did not, in fact, possess. "Yes?"

Julia stood there in her tightly cinched dressing gown, draped in moral superiority. Covered from head to toe as if that alone absolved her of whatever mischief had led her here in the first place. The irony was almost delicious.

"You will not win him, you know."

Oh, for God's sake.

"Pardon?" Clare deadpanned, though she could already see where this was going. The sheer predictability of it made her stomach twist.

"You heard me," Julia said, voice dripping with sweet venom. "Lord Trentham. He's looking for a decent wife. Not a whore like you."

Oh, how lovely. A good, old-fashioned insult wrapped up in the delicate lace of propriety. Clare felt the heat rise in her chest, but instead of giving Julia the satisfaction of a reaction, she simply exhaled. A pitying smile tugged at her lips.

"Say that again," Clare said softly.

Julia's eyes flashed. "I said he's looking for a decent wife. You can never be that, and you know it."

Clare tilted her head, taking her time before responding, letting the silence stretch long enough to make Julia shift ever so slightly. Then she smiled.

"Oh, darling," she said, voice like silk. "How do you know he's not looking for a bit of fun? Because we both know you couldn't manage that if you tried."

Julia gasped, scandalized, but Clare didn't stay to watch the indignation spread across her face. She turned, opened her door, and shut it firmly behind her, a slow, satisfied smile spreading across her lips.

Ah, it was lovely to picture Julia standing outside her door, wrapped in virtue but seething with rage.

CHAPTER TWELVE

Clare stood beside Meredith and Griffin on the gravel drive, the crisp morning air swirling around them as the last of the guests departed. Across the carriage-lined courtyard, the disappointed debutantes clutched their embroidered reticules and bid their farewells, their smiles polite but unmistakably forced.

It was quite sad. A parade of dashed hopes, really.

Each one had come to Southbury Hall with a single goal —to capture the attention of the elusive Marquess of Trentham. And each one had failed spectacularly.

Clare gave a particularly exuberant wave to Lady Julia, who pointedly ignored her as she climbed up into her carriage with her mother at her side.

"Poor things," Meredith murmured beside her, lifting a gloved hand in a farewell wave.

Clare hummed noncommittally, though she felt no real sympathy. The ladies who had spent the last several days angling for Ash's favor had done so with the same gleaming-eyed calculation the *ton* always applied to powerful, eligible men. None of them had cared much for Ash the man—only for Ashford Drake, the marquess. Ashford, the prize. They didn't know that he was a man who'd rescued a baby fox from a trap and set it free in the middle of a hunt. They didn't know that he treated his sister like gold and would do absolutely anything for her. They didn't know that he had three different sorts of smiles. One for when he was being wicked. One for when he was being playful, and one for when he was truly amused. And that of the three of them, she most coveted the third.

They didn't know Ash like she'd come to know him over the years. More than the older brother of her close friend, but as a man who wore a carefully cultivated mask around the people he didn't know or trust. A man who didn't allow the *ton* to see his true nature in precisely the same manner she had never allowed them to see hers. She understood him. The silly debutantes at the party this week, including Lady Julia? They didn't even know him.

And none of them had stood a chance.

Not when Ash had been far too busy burning her alive with his gaze.

She'd been honest with him. Nothing more *could* happen between them, and they both knew it. She wasn't being coy. She was being truthful. But she couldn't help the butterflies that winged through her middle when she thought about the look he'd given her last night in the study. He'd told her that her presence at Meredith's house in London would be an unholy temptation. It had taken all of her strength to turn and leave the room last night. Seeing him again in London might just break her.

As if summoned by thought alone, the great doors of the house opened, and there he was.

Ash strode down the stone steps, looking as infuriatingly handsome as ever. His dark hair was slightly tousled from the morning breeze, his gray eyes glinting with amusement as he approached. If the gaggle of debutantes had been hoping for one last glance, he gave them nothing more than a vague nod of farewell.

The moment the last carriage trundled through the gates, Meredith whirled on her brother with a look of utter betrayal.

"Ash, really." She let out a dramatic sigh. "You could have at least *feigned* interest in one of them."

Clare bit the inside of her cheek to keep from laughing.

"I did feign interest," Ash replied easily, scrunching up his nose. "Just not very well, apparently."

Griffin let out a low chuckle. "I did warn you, love," he said to Meredith, draping an arm lazily around her waist. "Your brother is hopeless."

"Hopeless," Meredith agreed. Then, narrowing her eyes at Ash, she added, "But let's not forget, dear brother, you lost the bet with Griffin last year. You *must* take a bride before your thirty-first birthday."

Clare's stomach twisted at the words.

She already knew about the bet. Everyone in their circle did. If Ash wasn't married by his next birthday, he'd forfeit something—land, money, perhaps a favorite horse—she wasn't sure.

All she knew was that Ash had laughed off the consequences at the time.

And now, with the deadline looming?

He still wasn't taking it seriously.

Ash gave a mock sigh, pressing a hand to his chest as if wounded. "So cold, Meredith. *Must* is such a heavy-handed word."

Meredith scowled. "Oh, spare me."

But Clare barely heard her. Because at that exact moment, Ash turned his attention to her, and a slow, heated look passed between them.

It was barely a flicker—a moment that lasted only a breath—but Clare felt the burn of it everywhere.

She schooled her expression, biting back the smile that threatened to betray her.

Meredith, oblivious to the silent exchange, folded her arms. "You haven't seen the last of me and my matchmaking efforts." She lifted her chin defiantly and rested a hand upon her expanding middle. "I am *determined* to find you a bride before I'm forced into confinement."

Griffin groaned. "Darling, please. I beg you to let this go. I'll happily take Trentham's prize horse as forfeit."

"And I will happily give him to you," Ash replied. Then he grumbled, "Well, perhaps not happily, but *willingly*, at least."

"I absolutely will not let this go," Meredith snapped. Then, turning back to Ash, she pointed a finger at him. "Don't think I won't come looking for you in London and bring along a beautiful lady or two."

Ash lifted a brow. "In that case, I'll make it easy for you."

Clare pretended to study the landscape.

Meredith narrowed her eyes. "How easy?"

"I'll come visit you in London." He slid his hands into his coat pocket, then added, as if completely indifferent, "Say, every Thursday night? For dinner?"

Clare almost gasped. A weekly dinner? How would she ever be able to sit through such evenings? No doubt Ash would employ the same sort of heated looks he'd just given her. Oh, dear. Perhaps she could find an excuse to bow out.

Meredith seemed caught off guard too. Ash hated domestic things. He avoided intimate family dinners with the same fervor he avoided the marriage mart.

"You'll—" She blinked. "You'll come to dinner?"

He shrugged, all casual nonchalance. "Why not?"

Meredith beamed. "Yes, absolutely. Thursday night."

"I'm looking forward to it," Ash murmured.

But he wasn't looking at his sister.
He was looking at Clare.
And Clare knew.
That dinner wasn't about family obligations.
God help her. It was about her.

CHAPTER THIRTEEN

London, Thursday Night

Ash had spent the last four days trying to rid himself of his inexplicable, unhealthy, perhaps disastrous attraction to Clare Handleton.

And he had failed. Spectacularly.

He had fenced until his arms ached, boxed until his ribs were sore, and ridden through Hyde Park at a punishing pace, as if sheer physical exhaustion could drive her from his mind.

It hadn't.

Not even his weekly faro game at the club, surrounded by brandy, smoke, and the usual meaningless conversation, had done the trick.

Nothing worked.

Because Clare had said she was infatuated with him. And because he wanted to kiss her again. He couldn't stop thinking about either thing.

It was ridiculous. It was inconvenient. It was maddeningly frustrating. But it was true. And it was not simply the words themselves, but *the way she had said them*—that teasing lilt in her voice, the knowing gleam in her eyes. Like she'd *been keeping a delicious secret* and had finally decided to let him in on it.

She had meant it too. That much he was certain of.

And that knowledge had become a persistent, maddening itch he couldn't quite reach.

So here he was, arriving at Meredith's London town house on a Thursday evening, feeling like a damned fool for how much he wanted to see Clare again.

The butler showed him into the drawing room, and Ash made a valiant effort to appear relaxed. He poured himself a drink, leaned against the mantel, and told himself—*for the hundredth time*—that he needed to get this thing under control.

He lifted his chin, straightened his shoulders, and cleared his throat. He was a grown man, a marquess, a member of the peerage for Christ's sake. He should be able to quash his attraction to one beautiful female.

Then Clare entered the room, and control became a thing of the past.

She had changed.

Not just into evening attire, but into something altogether more dangerous.

Her gown was a deep, rich burgundy that clung sinfully to her curves, the neckline just low enough to make a man's thoughts turn wicked. Her golden hair was pulled up, but a few loose tendrils had escaped, curling softly at her nape.

She was, quite frankly, fucking stunning.

And the way she looked at him? Like she knew exactly what she was doing to him, making his cock ache unbearably.

"Lord Trentham," she greeted, amusement tinging the edges of her voice.

"Lady Clare," he drawled, setting down his glass. He should have bowed politely, but instead, he lingered—taking his time, letting his gaze drift lazily over her.

Her lips twitched. "You're staring."

"You make it rather difficult not to."

A breath. A pause. The crackle of tension between them.

And then she smiled. Slow. Knowing. *Teasing.*

God help him.

"You wanted to see me again," he murmured, stepping closer. It was a statement, not a question.

She tilted her head, studying him, and put a gloved hand to her throat. "Did I?" she drawled.

"Don't play coy."

She laughed softly, the sound sending heat straight through him. "And if I did? What do you intend to do about it?"

Ash parted his lips to reply...when the door swung open.

"There you are, Ash," Meredith's voice rang out. "I wondered if you'd actually make an appearance here tonight."

Ash turned smoothly, slipping back into his usual mask of indifference.

"And disappoint my sister?" he said, placing a hand to his chest in mock offense. "I wouldn't dream of it."

Meredith and Griffin both gave him wary looks from the corners of their eyes.

Clare, for her part, looked utterly unbothered.

The moment passed, and then the four of them were heading to the dining room, exchanging polite conversation about the weather, the *ton*'s latest social engagements, and the future arrival of Meredith and Griffin's child.

Ash should have been engaged in the discussion. He should have had a dozen witty remarks ready to fill any silence. He should have had a score of ready questions about his future nephew. And he *did* hope the baby was a boy. He'd bet quite a large sum on it at the club.

But all he could do was watch Clare.

The curve of her mouth as she sipped her wine. The way the candlelight made her skin glow. The subtle way she shifted in her seat, as if aware of his gaze, as if she felt this thing between them just as acutely as he did.

It was excruciating.

What the devil was the matter with him?

And when she finally excused herself to use the convenience, he waited precisely two entire minutes before setting down his napkin and following her.

Then he wandered around in the corridor like a lovesick schoolboy until she came around the corner again. The moment he spotted her, he acted on pure instinct.

He reached for her, pulling her swiftly into a nearby room and closing the door behind them.

"Well, that was subtle," Clare murmured, eyes alight with mischief.

Ash barely heard her.

Because she was so damn close now, the scent of her—warm, sweet, utterly intoxicating—making him dizzy.

And before he could talk himself out of it, he cupped her face and kissed her.

Hard.

She made a soft sound of surprise against his mouth, but then—God help him—she melted into him.

Her hands slid up his chest, fisting the fabric of his jacket, pulling him closer, as if she had wanted this just as badly as he had.

He angled her head back, deepening the kiss, tasting the lingering hint of wine on her lips.

It was nothing like their last kiss.

This was hotter, more desperate, more demanding.

This was the kind of kiss that started fires.

He was barely aware of his hands sliding down her back, pulling her flush against him, of the way her body fit against his so perfectly.

He was about to say something reckless, something utterly irrevocable, when she pulled back slightly, her breathing unsteady.

"Damn you. Why do you have to be so good at that?"

His breath was coming in hard bursts. "I was about to ask you the same question."

"You still want to see me again?" she murmured.

His grip tightened. "You already know the answer to that."

Her lips parted slightly, as if considering something. Then —very deliberately—she tilted her head, watching him carefully, and asked, "Do you know the Onyx Club?"

The breath left his body.

Ash stilled, his entire body going taut.

Of course, he knew the Onyx Club.

It was a sin club. A pleasure club. A club where London's elite went to indulge in all sorts of wicked behavior.

And he, of course, was a longtime member.

His fingers flexed against her waist. He should have expected this from her. Clare had been full of surprises since the moment she walked into his life.

But this?

This changed everything.

CHAPTER FOURTEEN

The Onyx Club was everything the whispered rumors promised it to be—dark, decadent, and entirely without morals. Clare had been here before, many times, but never with the purpose she had tonight.

Black and gold adorned every surface, from the plush carpets beneath her slippered feet to the gilded chandeliers overhead, casting flickering light over the masked figures that lounged, drank, and gambled their inhibitions away.

Upstairs, behind locked doors and velvet curtains, the most elite members of the *ton* indulged in every sort of pleasure.

She had heard of this place from Marsden, of all people. That smug, selfish bastard had enjoyed boasting about his secret haunts, assuming she would be shocked and scandalized.

Instead, she had been intrigued. Little did Marsden know that telling her about the club would lead to her eventual freedom from the invisible shackles she'd worn since he'd tossed her aside.

Oh, yes, Clare had been here before. Many times. But always to gamble. Never to take a man upstairs.

Tonight, she intended to change that.

She adjusted the smooth black satin mask over her eyes and approached a roulette table, the hum of conversation surrounding her like an intoxicating spell.

The Onyx Club never failed to make her feel free. She was no stranger to scandal, to being whispered about behind fluttering fans with disapproving glances cast her way. But here at the club, there was no whispering save for wicked propositions. And judgment certainly had no place here. Reputation was something left outside the club's tall wooden doors. And that suited Clare just fine.

Normally, she came here to win large sums of money from drunken fools. The same types of drunken fools who rubbed elbows with odious men like the Earl of Marsden. She felt no guilt for taking their money at the end of the night. Half of the men she won from here were cheating both at cards and on their long-suffering wives. If she managed to make their purses lighter before they went back home, so be it.

And Clare had only a few more wins to go. A bit more money to stash away before she would feel safe enough to implement her plan. As soon as she had the amount she desired, she intended to leave England, *and her unforgiving mother*, far behind.

Yes, normally, Clare came here to gamble. But tonight, she had another purpose in mind. A much more scandalous and no doubt much more pleasurable one. She'd given it a lot of thought over the last few days since seeing Trentham again at dinner. And she'd come to one conclusion: tonight she would have him.

After all, if the *ton* insisted on branding her a fallen woman, why shouldn't she enjoy the fall?

And if she was going to risk everything again for a night of pleasure, there was only one man who had ever made her burn before he had even touched her.

Ashford Drake.

Of course, this could never be anything more. Marriage was unthinkable, and even an ongoing affair was too great a risk. She had too much to lose—most of all, her heart.

But pleasure? One night of pure, unforgettable pleasure?

That was entirely within reach. And the more she considered it, the more she craved it.

She'd only ever had Marsden's sweating, pawing grunts to go by. That was no memory to carry for a lifetime. But Ash… Ash would be different. She knew it instinctively. She could tell by the way he touched her, by the control in his kiss, the barely leashed lust in his smoldering eyes when he looked at her. He would make it good for her. Of that, she had no doubt. She was in for a treat tonight. And she was *greatly* looking forward to it.

She placed her bet—a careless flick of the wrist, sapphire-gloved fingers tossing a single golden chip onto the red twenty-one.

Then she felt him.

The presence at her back—heat, awareness, a pull so visceral it stole her breath.

Her lips curved into a half-smile.

"Are you stalking me, my lord?" she murmured without turning.

A deep chuckle, low and rich as sin.

"I had a suspicion you might be up to something interesting," Ash drawled. "Imagine my surprise to find you here."

She turned then, catching sight of him. Of course, they had planned to meet here tonight, but it was more entertaining to act as if it was merely a chance encounter. Like the rest of the patrons, they both wore masks, allowing them to slip into the illusion of being someone else, if only for a little while.

She let her gaze travel over him with deliberate appreciation.

Damn.

The Marquess of Trentham was already a dangerously handsome man, but here—in all black, his broad shoulders framed by the dark cut of his evening coat, his mask obscuring just enough of his features to make him look even more wicked than usual—he was devastating.

His eyes, stormy and knowing, watched her from behind his mask, the silver-gray catching the candlelight as he tilted his head in amused assessment.

He was every bit the rake and the predator, and tonight, she wanted to be hunted.

"Tell me," he continued smoothly, allowing his gaze to dip obviously to her *décolletage*, "do you always dress like a sapphire gemstone come to life when you gamble, or is this just for me?"

Clare let a slow smile curl her lips. "I suppose that depends."

"On?"

"Whether you like it."

His gaze darkened. "You already know the answer to that."

A thrill shot through her, low and deep. She pressed her thighs together, already aching for him.

The croupier called the spin, the ball rattling against the wheel, and they both turned to watch.

Clare's number hit.

The table erupted in murmurs and a few begrudging claps, but Clare barely noticed.

Not when Ash was still looking at her like that.

Like he wanted to drag her upstairs right then and there.

Clare collected her winnings, slipping them into the small satin reticule at her wrist.

Ash lifted a brow. "I believe I owe you congratulations."

She tilted her head. "Feeling generous?"

"I was about to offer to buy you a drink," he murmured, stepping just a little closer. "But I suspect what I really want isn't on the menu."

A sharp wave of heat shot through her. "Is that so?" she breathed.

His lips curved in that slow, wicked way that always made her stomach twist. "Tell me, Clare," he said, voice low and intimate. "Are you here to win at the tables?"

She met his gaze, heat simmering between them. "Not tonight."

His fingers brushed just along the inside of her wrist. A tease, a question, a promise.

"Then tell me," he murmured, his voice dropping even lower, his breath warm against her ear. "What, exactly, *do* you want?"

CHAPTER FIFTEEN

Ash hadn't planned on this. Hadn't planned on *her*—on Clare Handleton appearing in his life like a slow-burning match, igniting something he had no hope of controlling.

But he had stopped trying to fight it.

Tonight, there was no pretense, no teasing deflections. She had come here for him.

And he was about to give her everything she wanted. Everything *he* wanted as well.

With nothing more than a look, he procured a key from one of the barkeeps, slipping a coin into the man's hand before turning back to Clare. He held up the key between two fingers, watching the way her gaze flickered toward it— toward him.

He didn't ask her to follow.

He didn't need to.

She already had.

As they climbed the stairs, their eyes smoldered at each other, the tension between them taut as a bowstring. She was silent, but her breath quickened slightly when he led her down the dimly lit hallway, past gilded sconces and heavy doors that concealed the secrets of the *ton*'s most immoral elite.

He stopped at room ten. Turned the key in the lock. Pushed open the door.

And then, before they stepped inside, he turned to her, his arms wrapped around her waist, his voice a dark whisper at her ear. "Are you certain?"

Clare held his gaze, no hesitation in her eyes, only hunger and something else—something that mirrored the ache inside him.

"Yes," she murmured.

That was all he needed.

The moment the door closed behind them, he pushed her roughly back against it. His hands tangled in her hair, tilting her head back as his mouth claimed hers, hot and unrelenting. She kissed him back with equal fervor, fingers digging into his waistcoat, pulling him closer, as if she couldn't get enough—as if she had been waiting for this just as long as he had.

He turned her then and walked her backward until her spine met the far wall, pinning her there with the weight of his body.

"My…appetites are dark," he murmured against her lips.

She exhaled a breathless laugh. "You think you'll scare me off?"

His brow arched. "You've been warned."

Her fingers curled around the lapels of his coat, yanking him even closer.

"Try me."

Damn her. That was his last attempt. The last bit of valor in him to try to get her to run away from here, run away from him. Even though something deep inside of him already knew she wouldn't leave. Not now. She wanted him as much as he wanted her. And he was nearly mad with it.

He kissed her again, harder this time, stealing the breath from her lungs. His hands captured her wrists, pressing them above her head, securing them against the wall as he devoured her, lips and teeth and tongue, leaving her gasping beneath him.

She was fire. He was lost.

His hands slid downward, fisting in the fabric of her skirts, pulling them up in one smooth motion.

He found her beneath her shift, his fingers brushing against her silken heat.

And when he touched her—when he discovered she was already wet for him—his control snapped.

He lifted a brow, his breath uneven.

"What can I say?" she whispered, her voice full of wicked challenge. "I suppose I like dark."

Fuck.

His fingers slid inside her, and she moaned, head tipping back against the wall, eyes fluttering shut.

Ash watched her.

Watched the way her lips parted, the way her body arched into him, the way she lost herself completely in his hands.

He kissed her again, swallowing her sounds, then moved to her ear, his voice a husky command. "I'm going to touch you. All I want. And you're not allowed to make a sound. Do you understand?"

She nodded, biting her lip.

"Not words," he reminded her. "Nod."

She nodded again, her breath coming hard and fast.

Ash curled his fingers inside her, watching the way she struggled for control, her lip caught between her teeth, her chest rising and falling in sharp little gasps.

"Oh, yes, sweetheart," he growled against her ear. "Let me see it on your face."

She trembled beneath him.

"You want me?"

A nod. A whimper.

"You want more?"

Another nod, more frantic this time.

He pressed his forehead to hers, breathing her in.

"Have you ever climaxed standing up?" he murmured. "Against a wall?"

A tiny shake of her head.

He smiled. "Ah. Then let's do that, shall we?"

Clare stilled her hips, eyes dark with desire and trust.

And that trust—that was what undid him.

He had spent his entire life indulging in pleasure with women who knew the game, who played by the same rules, who never expected more than what he was willing to give.

But Clare—she wasn't just a conquest, wasn't just another night to be forgotten.

She was a risk.

A dangerous, beautiful risk.

And God help him, he was willing to take it.

"Keep your hands here," he instructed, releasing her wrists and dropping to his knees before her.

She gasped softly, tipping forward slightly, her fingers splaying backwards against the wall, wrists bent to steady herself.

He pushed up her skirts, his hands bracing her thighs, parting them just enough to claim her completely. She was beautiful, all pink and hot and wet and wanting. He breathed in her maddening scent, his cock so hard it hurt.

And then—he tasted her.

The first stroke of his tongue sent a violent tremor

through her, her thighs quivering as she gasped, whimpered, struggled to stay silent.

He didn't stop.

He licked and teased, his fingers sliding inside her in a slow, relentless rhythm.

She bucked against him, and he held her down, a rough hand gripping her hip, keeping her steady as he brought her higher and higher, watching the pleasure break across her face.

When she shattered, she didn't stay silent.

She cried out, her fingernails digging into the wall, her body writhing beneath his lips as he devoured every last tremor of her release.

Ash finally stood, wiping his mouth with the back of his hand. He arched a brow. "You weren't quiet."

Clare panted, her face flushed, her body still trembling. "I know," she breathed. Then—gathering herself, regaining her control—she lifted her chin and met his gaze. "What are you going to do about it?" she murmured, eyes dark and daring. "Punish me?"

Christ.

Ash's control snapped all over again.

Clare barely had time to catch her breath before Ash surged forward, pressing her back against the wall again, his body caging hers in. His hands gripped her waist, firm and unyielding, holding her exactly where he wanted her. The wicked gleam in his storm-gray eyes sent a shiver through her—anticipation, thrill, and something far darker.

"You asked me what I was going to do about your little disobedience." His voice was a low, deliberate rasp, sending heat curling through her belly. He reached up, sliding his fingers along her throat, his thumb resting against her pulse point. It thundered under his touch, betraying her excitement.

"I should leave you aching for it," he mused, tilting his head as if considering. "Make you beg."

Clare swallowed hard, but she refused to look away. "You could," she admitted, lips lifting into a wicked smile. "But we both know you won't."

His eyes darkened, the ghost of a smirk playing at his lips. "You're right," he murmured, brushing his mouth over her jaw, teasing her with the barest graze of his lips. "I want to hear you beg, but not because I make you. I want you to lose yourself so completely that you can't help but fall apart for me."

She exhaled sharply as he gripped the fabric of her gown, gathering the skirts in his hands before lifting her off the floor in one swift motion. She gasped, instinctively wrapping her legs around his waist. His strength, his sheer control, sent a fresh wave of arousal crashing through her.

"Ash—"

"Not a sound unless I tell you to make one," he ordered, his voice deep and commanding.

She shuddered at the authority in it, her nails digging into his shoulders.

His mouth found hers then, searing, consuming, as he carried her to the bed. The kiss was a claiming, his tongue parting her lips, tasting, taking, his grip on her tightening as if he had no intention of letting go. When the backs of her knees hit the mattress, he lowered her down, following her, never breaking contact.

He made quick work of her gown, dragging it over her head, baring her to him. He took a slow, appreciative breath, his eyes drinking her in. The reverence in his gaze made her skin flush, made her pulse skitter.

"You are exquisite," he murmured, running his knuckles along the slope of her breast.

She arched into his touch, desperate for more, but he was in no rush. He trailed his fingers lower, tracing the curve of her hip, then lower still. When his hand finally pressed between her thighs, she moaned, unable to stop herself.

His fingers stroked her, teasing, testing, slipping through her slick heat. He let out a low, approving sound. "Already so wet for me again," he mused. "Tell me, Clare, is this for me?"

"Yes," she gasped, hips tilting toward his hand, desperate for more.

"Good," he murmured, rewarding her with a deep stroke of his fingers, his touch firm, unrelenting. She clenched around him, the pressure coiling low, unbearable and perfect all at once. But just as the pleasure built to a peak, he withdrew, his hand leaving her aching and empty.

She let out a soft whimper, her body protesting the loss.

He caught her chin between his fingers, tilting her face up. "I told you, love," he said, his voice rich with amusement and wicked promise. "You don't get to come until I say so."

She bit her lip, equal parts frustration and desperate need swirling inside her. "Then don't make me wait too long."

His eyes flashed with something primal. "You don't get to make demands here," he murmured, pressing a hot, open-mouthed kiss to the column of her throat. "But I'll give you what you need. When I'm ready."

Clare's breath hitched as he moved lower, trailing kisses down her body, his lips and tongue branding her with every touch. When he settled between her thighs, she barely had a moment to brace herself before his mouth found her.

Her fingers fisted in the sheets, her body arching off the mattress as he licked into her with slow, devastating precision. He feasted on her, his tongue stroking, teasing, driving her to the very edge of madness. Every flick, every deliberate swirl sent fire rushing through her veins.

And then he stopped.

She nearly sobbed at the loss.

Ash lifted his head, his eyes burning into hers. "Not yet," he murmured.

She whimpered, trembling beneath him. "Ash… Please."

His smirk was pure sin. "That's what I wanted," he murmured. "You begging for it."

He rose above her then, shifting her beneath him, his

hands gripping her thighs, positioning her exactly how he wanted. He unfastened his breeches, his movements slow, deliberate, as if savoring her helpless anticipation. When he finally pressed against her, his thick length teasing at her entrance, she let out a ragged moan, her entire body strung tight with need.

"Look at me," he commanded, his voice rough.

She obeyed, her gaze locking onto his.

Then, in one slow, unyielding thrust, he pushed inside her, seating himself to the hilt.

A sharp gasp tore from her throat. He was thick, filling her completely, stretching her in the most devastating way. She clenched around him, her nails biting into his back as she struggled to catch her breath.

Ash groaned, his head dropping to her shoulder. "Bloody hell, Clare."

She trembled beneath him, her entire body alight with sensation. "Move," she breathed. "Please."

He lifted his head, his gaze molten as he pulled back, then thrust into her again, harder this time.

And then there was nothing but pleasure.

He set a punishing rhythm, driving into her with deep, claiming strokes. Each thrust sent white-hot bliss spiraling through her, pulling her closer and closer to the edge. She could hear the ragged sound of their breathing, the way his name tore from her lips, the dark praise he whispered in her ear as he took her apart piece by piece.

"So tight for me," he growled, his grip on her hips tightening. "You feel like heaven, love."

She could only moan in response, her body tightening around him, chasing that peak, desperate to fall over the edge.

Ash felt it. He slowed, grinding into her, angling his hips until—

"Oh— God," she gasped, her vision going white.

"Now," he ordered, his voice thick with command. "Come for me, Clare."

And she shattered.

The pleasure crashed over her, hot and overwhelming, her body shaking beneath him as she convulsed around his length. Ash groaned, thrusting deep one last time, his own release following hers, his body rigid as he spilled inside her.

For a long moment, the only sound in the room was their ragged breathing, the pounding of their hearts against each other's skin.

Then, slowly, Ash lifted himself just enough to press a lingering kiss to her lips. It was softer now, less urgent, but no less claiming.

Clare sighed, her fingers drifting lazily along his back. "I think I've been thoroughly punished."

Ash chuckled, nipping at her lower lip. "Oh, darling," he murmured. "That wasn't your punishment."

Her breath caught as he rolled her beneath him once more, a wicked grin curving his lips.

"That," he said, voice husky with promise, "is just the beginning."

CHAPTER SEVENTEEN

Clare lay tangled in warm, rumpled sheets, her body utterly wrecked in the best possible way. Her limbs felt boneless, her skin flushed, her breath still coming in lazy, satisfied waves.

Three times.

She had told herself this would be one night, *one time*, enough to exorcise the years-long infatuation she had carried for Ash.

But once hadn't been enough.

Not even close.

She turned her head on the pillow to look at him, this man who had completely undone her.

Ash lay beside her, one arm draped behind his head, the other lazily tracing patterns over her bare hip. His gray eyes, hooded with satisfaction, met hers, and that damned smirk tugged at his lips.

"You're staring," he murmured.

"You're smug," she shot back.

He laughed, shifting slightly so he could prop himself up

on one elbow. "I've just spent the last few hours thoroughly ruining you. Can you blame me?"

Heat flashed through her all over again at the memory of exactly how thoroughly he had done so.

She bit her lip, forcing herself to focus on something else —anything else—before she forgot herself entirely and climbed back on top of him.

Ash's fingers idly traced her thigh. "Why did you want to meet here tonight?"

She allowed a sensual smile to curl her lips. "Isn't it obvious?"

He slowly dragged his tongue over his bottom lip. "No. I mean. Why risk another scandal?"

She sighed and dropped her head back onto the pillow. "The first time I ruined my reputation for nothing. There was absolutely no pleasure in coupling with Marsden."

Ash nearly choked on a laugh. "I don't doubt it."

"If I'm to be ruined, I wanted to experience pleasure at least once."

Ash cleared his throat. "It was *three times*…and counting."

She tossed a pillow at his head. He caught it and gave her an unrepentant grin. "So?"

She arched a brow. "So what?"

"*Ahem*, I do hope I didn't disappoint."

"Fishing for a compliment, my lord?"

"Never." He dragged his fingers up her thigh again and chuckled. Then he fell back against the mattress, clutching the pillow to his chest. "Where do you suppose your mother thinks you are at this very moment?"

Clare exhaled a slow breath, blinking up at the ceiling. "She usually leaves me alone when I'm staying with Meredith."

He nodded, letting his fingers trace little circles on her hip. "And when you're not?"

"When I'm not," she said, voice dry, "I'm at home in the countryside with her. Where she provides me with nearly constant condemnation."

"Truly?" Ash asked, his brow crumpling into a frown.

"Oh, yes. She never allows me to forget for a moment that I've ruined the family." She let out a loud, long sigh. "At least I am an only child. I should hate to have ruined a sibling as well. I doubt I could handle that guilt."

Ash's hand stilled on her skin.

"She shouldn't treat you like that," he said, his tone sharp with quiet disapproval.

Clare laughed, though the sound was humorless. "As if I have a choice," she murmured. "As if I have a choice about *anything*—how I'm treated by my mother, by Society." She turned her head to look at him. "This is my choice. Tonight is my choice."

His gaze darkened.

And then—just like that—the tension between them shifted.

Ash moved swiftly, rolling her onto her back, his bare weight pressing against her.

"Then by all means," he murmured, lips ghosting over hers, his voice all heat and promise. "Let's do it again."

She gasped as he captured her mouth, their bodies already moving together, desire flaring white-hot between them once more.

CHAPTER EIGHTEEN

The Next Day, Gentleman Jack's Boxing Saloon

The rhythmic thud of fists against leather echoed through the saloon, the air thick with sweat, exertion, and the lingering haze of cigar smoke from the men watching from the benches along the walls.

Ash drove his fist into the practice bag again, his bare knuckles smarting against the leather. It wasn't enough.

Nothing was enough.

He had spent all night tangled in Clare Handleton's body, his hands on her skin, his mouth at her throat, his name on her lips as she came apart beneath him—and yet here he was, aching for her all over again.

It should have been enough. It should have burned her out of his system.

Instead, it had only made things worse.

"Let's go," Southbury called, already circling in the ring, rolling his shoulders as he prepared for another round.

Ash strode over to face his friend, his fists at the ready.

"You're distracted," Southbury said flatly. "And when you're distracted, you're sloppy."

Ash scowled, lifting his fists. "Sloppy, am I?"

Southbury lifted his brows. "Prove me wrong."

Ash swung, a sharp jab, then a follow-up uppercut that Griffin barely dodged. The duke let out a low chuckle, shaking his head. "There's that temper. I thought perhaps you'd be aiming it at your sister after she read you the riot act the other night for failing to find a bride at the house party."

"The house party. Ugh." Ash grunted. "Don't remind me."

Southbury arched a brow. "Still planning to give me that horse of yours?"

"I don't see why Meredith is so set on marrying me off," Ash said with narrowed eyes.

"Perhaps she wants our child to have cousins," Southbury replied with a grin.

"Isn't Gemma going to have a baby? There's a cousin for you."

Southbury shook his head.

The two continued sparring, moving in tight, controlled circles. The rhythmic pounding of flesh against flesh and heavy breathing was the only sound between them for a while.

Finally, as they broke apart to catch their breath, Ash wiped the sweat from his brow and asked, far too casually, "What do you think about Clare Handleton?" *Damn.* He hadn't intended to be that blunt, but the question had practically leaped from his lips.

Southbury gave him a sharp look as he adjusted his stance. "What about her?"

Ash shrugged, attempting nonchalance. "You and Meredith have known her for years."

Griffin exhaled, lowering his fists slightly. "Yes. It's a

damn shame what happened to her. If I ever spot Marsden in a dark alley alone, I cannot be held responsible for what might happen to that blackguard."

"I only hope I'm there with you when it happens," Ash growled.

Griffin continued, "Meredith adores Clare, you know. And with good reason. She's loyal, steadfast, whip smart. She's one of the few people who's ever been completely honest with my wife, and that's a rare thing in our world."

Loyal. Steadfast. Whip smart.

Ash swallowed hard.

All words that described Clare exactly.

Last night she had also been wicked and wild and completely uninhibited, pressing herself against him, daring him to do his worst, matching him stroke for stroke, moan for moan. It had been the most satisfying sexual experience of his life.

His stomach tightened at the memory.

He could still taste her.

Could still feel the imprint of her body beneath his hands.

And yet, despite all of that—despite everything they had done behind locked doors at the Onyx Club—she still had to live under the double standard that ruled their Society.

Nothing had happened to Marsden after he had ruined her.

Yet Clare was an outcast.

And to make matters worse, Clare had to endure her self-righteous mother's constant belittling, as if she had any control over how the world had decided to see her.

It wasn't fair. Damn it.

And Ash hated unfair things.

And for the first time, a thought—a dangerous, mad thought—took root in his mind.

Perhaps there could be more between us.

The idea hit him with the force of a well-placed punch to the gut.

He nearly staggered with it.

No.

That was insane.

He wasn't the marrying kind. He wasn't even the courting kind.

And even if he were, it wouldn't be *with Clare*. It couldn't be with Clare, for reasons that had nothing to do with her sullied reputation. *If* he were to marry, he would need a wife who would let him be. Leave him alone while he did as he wanted. Clare would never be that sort of wife. He already knew that about her. He'd make her miserable.

Wouldn't he?

"Why are you asking about Clare?" Southbury's voice cut through Ash's tangled thoughts, snapping him back to the present.

"Oh, er, uh… no reason." It sounded unconvincing, even to his own ears. He was never that ineloquent.

Southbury arched a brow, clearly suspicious. "Was there a reason you danced with her at the house party?" he pressed. "Other than nearly giving my poor pregnant wife a fit," the duke drawled.

A slow, devilish smile curved Ash's lips. "I would *never* endanger my dear sister's health."

"Then why *did* you ask Clare to dance?"

Ash's smirk deepened. "Because a beautiful lady deserves to dance," he said smoothly, his tone light but laced with something else—something unreadable. Then after a beat, he added with a glint in his eye, "especially when she's spent far too long standing on the edges of the ballroom."

CHAPTER NINETEEN

Clare sat on the edge of her bed, her fingers toying with the folded slip of vellum in her lap. She had read it three times now, the single word written in Ash's bold, slanted script—it was vague, but she knew exactly what he was asking.

Again?

Her body still thrummed with the memory of his touch, the way he had commanded her, unraveled her, put her back together again. It had been blistering. It had been reckless. And it had been exactly what she needed.

But it could never happen again.

Another scandal wouldn't just ruin her further—it would destroy her. Her mother had made that clear. If she embarrassed the family again, if she drew any more whispers, there would be no mercy. She would be sent away to a convent, and this time, the threat wasn't idle. Her mother had mentioned it more than once, and Clare knew she would follow through.

Living with her mother was unbearable, but at least she could sneak away and steal moments of freedom. A convent though? Nuns watching her every move, judging, suffocating? The thought alone made her shudder. No. She needed to win the last bit of money necessary for her to leave the country. And the sooner the better. Once her mother came to fetch her in a fortnight, she wouldn't have another chance to return to London until spring.

She sighed, pressing the vellum flat against her palm. She could say yes. She could go to him again, lose herself in him again, let him ruin her in the most delicious ways.

But that would be foolish.

She was already walking the razor's edge of scandal. She had got what she wanted—what she had craved for years. A taste of Ashford Drake. An unforgettable coupling. And it had been glorious.

Now, she needed to stop before she lost herself entirely.

She picked up a quill, hesitated for only a moment, then scribbled her reply.

No.

She folded the note, sealing it carefully before handing it off to a footman with a good coin and instructions to ensure it reached Lord Trentham without delay. As the door shut behind the servant, Clare exhaled, steadying herself.

She had done the right thing.

So why did it feel like she had just set fire to the one thing that had ever made her feel truly alive?

CHAPTER TWENTY

Ash read the note again, the one word pressing into his mind like an imprint.

No.

A wry, humorless laugh escaped him. He was not a man accustomed to refusals. Women never turned him away—at least, not until now.

But Clare had.

Clare, who had melted beneath his touch, whispered his name like a prayer, met his passion with her own. He knew the difference between affection and mere indulgence, and what had passed between them had been real.

So why was she walking away?

His fingers tightened around the note, not in anger, but in frustration. He had never needed to chase anyone before, had never wanted to. But this—*she*—was different.

If she truly wished to sever whatever was between them, he would respect that. He had to. But he needed to know—

was that what she truly wanted? Or was she simply afraid? Of scandal, of gossip, of whatever burden she believed would come from being with him?

He would give her a choice. A moment of honesty, face to face. No demands, no ultimatums. Just a chance to tell him, without hesitation, whether she wished to be free of him.

And if she did?

Then he would walk away.

Because whatever else burned inside him—desire, longing, something perilously close to devotion—one truth mattered above all.

Clare Handleton was not his to claim.

She was only ever his if she wished to be.

But he couldn't let her go without one more try.

CHAPTER TWENTY-ONE

Clare sat across from Ash in Meredith's drawing room, tension winding between them like an unspoken challenge. The butler had served their tea and, at her insistence, left the door open as he withdrew. Even that felt too much. Too intimate.

"You expect me to believe that you just *happened* to visit your sister when she's out paying her weekly calls?" she asked, carefully pouring cream into her teacup.

Ash's own tea sat untouched beside him. He lifted a shoulder in a lazy shrug. "I thought she was no longer making visits in her condition."

"She has a few more weeks yet," Clare replied smoothly.

"Ah. I see." His voice was mild, almost indifferent. But Clare knew better. This was no coincidence.

She should never have come down to the drawing room.

She had refused him at first, had sent the butler back again and again with firm denials. But after Spaulding's third return—flustered and informing her that Lord Trentham refused to leave—she had relented.

Now, faced with Ash in an otherwise empty house, she knew she had made a mistake.

She stirred her tea vigorously, focusing on the rhythmic clink of the spoon against porcelain, trying desperately to ignore how very good he looked in his casual buckskin breeches, white shirt, and emerald waistcoat. "You might as well say what you came to say."

Ash leaned forward. "Why won't you see me again?"

Her fingers tightened around the spoon. "Lower your voice," she hissed, casting a glance toward the open door.

"I don't care if anyone hears," he said flippantly.

"Well, I do." She shot him a sharp look.

He exhaled through his nose, as if reining in impatience. "Fine," he whispered. "But tell me—why?"

She set her spoon down, her hands deliberately still. "Because I cannot."

His jaw tightened. "Cannot, or will not?"

She let out a breath, barely above a whisper. "Does it matter?"

"Yes."

She shook her head, staring down at her tea. "We both know this is impossible."

"I know it's not wise," he corrected, viciously scrubbing a hand through his hair. "That's not the same thing."

"You're making light of something quite serious."

His eyes darkened. "You think this isn't serious to me?"

She met his gaze, trying to summon detachment. "I think you are a man accustomed to saying whatever is necessary to get what he wants."

Without hesitation, he slid from his chair to kneel before her, capturing her hand in his. "I am saying this because it is the truth. I cannot stop thinking about you."

"Get up," she insisted, panic flashing through her. If the

butler returned, or if a maid happened by—God, what would they think?

"Not until you look at me and see how goddamned serious I am."

Her breath caught as their gazes locked. There in his expression, in the quiet intensity of his eyes—she saw it.

He meant it.

Damn him.

"All right," she whispered. "I believe you."

Something flickered in his expression, relief and something deeper. "Do you?"

"Yes," she said, firmer now. "Now, for God's sake, get up."

With a measured breath, he rose and smoothed a hand down his waistcoat, regaining his composure. "It's true. I haven't been able to stop thinking about you. If you can honestly say you haven't thought of me since that night at the club, I will leave."

She closed her eyes. "I want to say it."

"But you can't?"

A groan of frustration escaped her as she pushed to her feet, pacing toward the window. "Why are you doing this?"

He followed, his presence a heat at her back. "I am not in control of it any more than you are."

She turned to face him, squaring her shoulders. "Very well. I do need to go to the Onyx Club again."

His brows pulled together. "Why?"

"I have my reasons."

"What reasons?" His gaze narrowed on her face.

She shook her head. "That is not the point."

He studied her, frustration tightening his jaw. "When?"

She hesitated. "Saturday night."

Something shifted in his expression, the tension easing just slightly.

"If you are there…" She glanced away and drew in a steadying breath. "So be it."

He let out a long exhale, closing his eyes briefly before meeting hers again. She had not given him what he wanted. Not exactly.

But she had given him enough.

CHAPTER TWENTY-TWO

Saturday Night, The Onyx Club

The Onyx Club was alight with the blaze of a thousand candles hanging from the golden chandeliers that graced the ceiling of the large space. It was a tempest of sound and sin, alive with laughter, filled with people indulging in their worst impulses. Drinking, gambling, seducing—giving in to the recklessness that Society claimed to abhor yet secretly craved.

Clare had long since learned to keep to the shadows. Even here, in a place where rules were made to be broken, she preferred not to be seen. Tonight was no exception.

She had done well at faro. More than well. Now, she turned her luck to the roulette table, playing the numbers Marsden had whispered to her once—the ones that his scheming cohorts had ensured would land more often than not on this particular table. A trick. A deception. But the world had deceived her first, hadn't it?

If someone had told her eleven years ago that she would one day be sitting in a club like this, slipping past the edges of Society to cheat at games of chance with plans to escape the country, she would have laughed in their face.

Now, she didn't laugh.

She just kept playing.

And then—she felt him.

The air around her changed. It grew warmer, tighter, like the space itself recognized his presence before she had even turned her head.

She looked up.

Their eyes locked across the room.

Ash.

He wore black again. Of course he did. As if he needed to look any more dangerous, any more ruinous. Storm-gray eyes cutting through her, stripping her down to the place inside her that still burned for him.

Because she did burn for him.

She had tried to forget. Tried to pretend the memory of him—the way he had moved against her, inside her, the way he had murmured her name like it belonged only to him— did not take up so much space in her memory.

But it did.

And the way he looked at her now told her he knew it.

She was wearing red tonight. A foolish choice. Red was for women who wanted to be seen. She had spent years perfecting invisibility, and yet she had worn the one color that made her impossible to ignore.

The ball spun, the wheel clattered, the croupier called the number.

She won.

Again.

She schooled her features into feigned surprise, playing the role of a woman delighted by luck. But Ash's gaze sharpened. He was perceptive, and now—he was wondering.

How was she winning so easily?

Her pulse pounded. She swept her winnings into her reticule and rose. She did not hurry. Did not flee. She walked with measured steps toward the bar.

But he was behind her in an instant.

She didn't turn. Didn't need to.

"I'd like a drink tonight," she said lightly.

His voice came from just behind her, low and familiar, roughened in a way that sent heat curling through her belly. "Brandy?"

"Champagne."

She slid onto a stool, ignoring the way her skin prickled in awareness of his nearness.

Ash ordered their drinks, his eyes never leaving her.

"Why did you come here tonight?" he asked.

"To gamble." The answer was immediate.

His brows furrowed. "I don't understand."

"I have plans." She met his gaze steadily. "Plans which require a certain amount of money."

He looked even more confused. "Money? Why do you need—"

She exhaled. The words came as evenly as she could manage. "I've nearly saved enough to leave England."

A beat of silence.

Then he said softly, almost disbelievingly, "What?"

She turned, leveling him with a look. "Lower your voice."

But his entire body had gone still. "You're leaving England?"

"Yes."

His jaw clenched. "Does Meredith know?"

"No. And I don't want her to. When my mother comes looking for me, I don't want Meredith to be forced to lie. Once I'm safe, I'll write."

His hands curled into fists against the bar. "Where will you go?"

"The Continent. Most likely France." She lifted her glass and took a slow sip. "They're more forgiving there." A ghost of a smile. "I intend to tell everyone I'm a widow."

His throat worked as he swallowed. "When?"

"As soon as I have enough."

She could feel his frustration mounting, the energy coiling between them like a gathering storm.

"I'm nearly there," she murmured, patting her reticule. "And I don't have much time. My mother is coming for me before the end of the month."

Something flashed in his expression—something she could not name.

"Why?" His voice was raw. "Why are you leaving?"

She arched a brow. "Would you stay in a Society that openly shuns you?"

His breath came rougher now. She could feel it more than see it.

He was upset.

And she—she was unraveling.

She had prepared for this conversation. Had thought herself ready to say the words and mean them. To walk away from him without looking back.

But the way he was looking at her now—like he wanted to consume her, like he wanted to stop time itself just to keep her here—made something inside her crack.

His voice was a quiet plea. "Come upstairs with me."

She should say no.

She should leave, flee into the night, never look back.

But his voice was in her blood, his hands already whispers against her skin, and against all sense, all reason, all the careful plans she had spent years making—

"Yes," she whispered.

And then his hand was in hers, pulling her toward ruin.

CHAPTER TWENTY-THREE

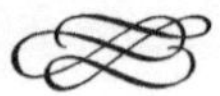

Ash had waited for this moment. Dreamed of it. Driven himself mad with the memory of her—her taste, her body beneath his, the way she had come apart in his arms.

And now, she was here again.

The door to room ten closed behind them with a quiet click. It might as well have been a thunderclap. Because the second they were alone, the second there was nothing between them but air and everything unsaid, Ash moved.

He caught her around the waist, pulling her against him, his mouth finding hers in a kiss that was all heat and hunger and, damn it, desperation.

Her fingers curled into his coat, but then—she pressed her hands against his chest, pushing him back.

He blinked, breathing hard, frowning.

"If we are to continue this, we must establish some rules first," she said, her voice low, measured. But her pupils were wide, her breath unsteady. She wanted him as badly as he wanted her. He could see it.

"Rules?" he echoed, shaking his head. "I don't understand."

"This—" She gestured between them, at the room, at the wicked anticipation thrumming in the air. "It can be nothing more than a distraction. A moment of pleasure. That is all."

He stepped forward, crowding her against the door, dragging his lips along her jaw, down her throat. She shivered.

"I thought that's exactly what it is," he murmured against her skin.

A breathless sigh escaped her lips, but she caught herself, tilting her chin up. "I'm serious, Ash," she said, though her voice had lost its edge. "You must promise me. No feelings. No entanglements."

"No feelings?" he repeated, catching her hand and guiding it downward, pressing her palm to the hard length of him beneath his breeches. "This is how I feel. Do you object?"

She made a strangled sound as he kissed the sensitive spot just below her ear.

But then… She forced herself to pull away.

Her eyes burned into his, her next words like a shot to the chest.

"No falling in love."

Ash stilled.

For the first time since stepping into this room, something in him stopped short, like a carriage horse rearing back at an unseen drop-off.

"Love?" He said the word as if it were foreign to him.

Her gaze flickered away. "I cannot continue this affair unless you agree." She swallowed hard, her chest rising and falling. "You must swear it."

Ash exhaled, dragging a hand through his hair, his body still tight with need. "No love," he said finally, the words feeling strange on his tongue. "Fine. I agree."

Relief crossed her face. "Good."

But as he took her in his arms again, as he stripped her bare, as he tied her wrists above her head and made her gasp his name, something dark and dangerous twisted in his chest.

Because, damn it all, love had never even crossed his mind.

Not until she told him it was impossible.

And now?

Now, it was all he could think about.

Oh, hell. He was so screwed.

CHAPTER TWENTY-FOUR

The next time they met at the club, there was no pretense. No veiled glances. No lingering innuendo. Just the quiet, thrilling understanding that had built between them, simmering beneath the surface for far too long.

Ash watched her from across the room, the flickering candlelight playing over her features as she played faro, winning round after round with effortless grace. But she wasn't looking at the cards. Not really. Every now and then, her gaze flicked to him—small, fleeting moments, but each one sent a pulse of heat through him.

And then, without a word, they left together.

Upstairs, the air between them was thick with expectation. As soon as the door shut behind them, she was in his arms, their bodies colliding with a force that had been held back for too long. Clare barely had time to gasp before Ash lifted her, carried her to the bed, and laid her down upon it. Firelight cast flickering shadows along the walls, painting her golden against the dark.

She arched a brow, breathless, teasing. "What took you so long?"

He locked the door with a soft click. "Two seconds is too long to be away from you." His voice was low, roughened by the hunger that had haunted him all evening.

She reached for him, but he was already moving, lowering himself onto the mattress beside her. His heat seeped into her skin before his lips ever touched her, and when they finally did—when he kissed her—she melted into him as if she had been waiting for this moment forever.

Her fingers tangled in his hair, pulling him closer, but it wasn't enough. She needed more.

Ash could see it in the way her chest rose and fell too quickly, the way her pupils were blown wide with something wild. But before he could claim her, she did something unexpected.

Leaning back against the pillows, she trailed one delicate hand down her body, her fingers skimming the curve of her waist before slipping lower.

His pulse thundered.

"Teasing me, love?" His voice was nothing but gravel.

She met his gaze, her eyes dark with challenge. "Would you prefer I didn't?"

His jaw clenched. God help him, but he had never been so desperate for a woman in his life.

With a sharp exhale, his hands went to the fall of his breeches, undoing the buttons with swift, impatient fingers. He was hard—achingly so—and the sight of her sprawled out before him, touching herself with unabashed confidence, made him throb with need.

Her moans filled the space between them, soft, breathless sounds that made his blood burn. When she reached for him, tugging him toward her, he didn't hesitate.

With one smooth thrust, he slid inside her, and the world tilted.

She gasped, her nails digging into his back as he stretched her, filled her, consumed her completely.

His control was razor-thin, but he wanted to make this last. He set a slow, deliberate rhythm, rolling his hips to feel every bit of her, to make her feel every inch of him. Her body arched to meet him, her legs wrapping around his waist, pulling him deeper, holding him in place as if she never wanted to let him go.

"Ash," she gasped, her voice breaking on his name.

He groaned against her skin, his lips trailing from her neck to her collarbone before finding her breast. He took a nipple into his mouth, teasing with his tongue, and the sound she made nearly undid him.

She was close. He could feel it in the way her body clenched around him, the way her breathing grew more erratic. But she wanted more.

With a sudden shift, she pushed against his chest, flipping them so she was on top, straddling him.

His breath caught. He never let women take control. Not ever.

But Clare—Clare was different.

She was fire and recklessness and temptation wrapped in golden skin, and as she sank down onto him, slow and deliberate, he thought he might go mad.

His hands gripped her hips, guiding her movements as she rocked against him, setting a pace that was both torturous and perfect.

Then she smiled.

That did it.

With a growl, his fingers found the delicate bundle of nerves at her core. The moment he touched her, she gasped, her rhythm faltering.

"Oh," she breathed, her head tilting back, pleasure washing over her features.

His smirk was pure sin. "You like that?"

"Yes," she panted. "Please."

"Please what?" His voice was dark, teasing.

"Please make me come."

That was all it took. His fingers moved in slow, devastating circles, pushing her higher, closer—until, with a sharp cry, she shattered.

The sight of her unraveling, her body clenching around him, was his undoing. He flipped her onto her back, driving into her with deep, urgent strokes. She was still trembling from her release, her body pulsing around him, and as she gasped his name, he followed her over the edge, groaning his pleasure against her lips.

For a long moment, neither of them moved.

Clare lay tangled beneath him, her golden hair spread across the pillows, her skin warm, her body still humming with pleasure.

Ash exhaled slowly, his forehead resting against hers.

He had never felt so utterly spent. Never been so completely satisfied.

And he had never been more terrified.

CHAPTER TWENTY-FIVE

The room was dark, the only light coming from the low embers in the fireplace. The remnants of their meal sat forgotten on the side table, the tray empty except for a few scattered crumbs and half-drunk glasses of wine.

But Clare barely noticed any of it.

She lay tangled in Ash's arms, their bodies still damp from the heat of their lovemaking. Her limbs were languid, her muscles pliant, her skin still singing with pleasure. She should have felt satisfied. She was satisfied. And yet…something restless coiled inside her, something she refused to name.

Ash had been the one to fetch the meal, making sure the barmaid who delivered it never caught a glimpse of Clare's face. She had appreciated the gesture more than she could say. It was thoughtful, considerate—which only made this entire situation more dangerous.

After eating, they'd returned to bed. But instead of taking each other again, instead of getting lost in the physical, something unexpected had happened.

They had talked.

Actually talked.

Ash lay beside her, his arm draped loosely over her waist, his fingers absently tracing shapes against her skin.

"Do you remember the time Lady Oxbridge's wig came off at the musicale?" he asked, his smile unguarded, real. The one she coveted.

Clare bit her lip to keep from bursting into laughter. "And her daughter had to chase it down the aisle as if it were a wayward kitten."

Ash let out a deep, rumbling laugh, shaking his head. "God, I had forgotten that part."

Clare was grinning so hard her cheeks hurt. When was the last time she had laughed like this?

Certainly not in the company of a man.

Her mirth faded slightly as she wiped a tear from the corner of her eye. "Lady Oxbridge, wigless at the musicale. And yet *I'm* the one Society shuns," she mused. "I hardly think it's fair."

Ash chuckled softly, but his humor didn't last long. His expression sobered, and a moment later, he reached out, running the back of his fingers along her jaw, as if memorizing the shape of her face.

"You didn't deserve what happened to you," he murmured.

Clare's throat tightened. She looked away. "No lady deserves to be shunned for the same sins men commit without consequence." She exhaled slowly. "But when has Society ever been fair?"

Silence stretched between them.

She risked a glance at Ash. Why did he have to be so damnably handsome? Why did he have to be charming and clever and—God help her—kind?

This would all be so much easier if he weren't.

She wasn't even certain why she'd insisted on the rule. *No falling in love.* Maybe she had been trying to protect him. Maybe she had been trying to protect herself.

But the awful, sinking feeling in her gut told her the truth.

The rule had been for her.

Because if she hadn't said it, if she hadn't put that safeguard in place, she would have fallen headfirst into something she couldn't control.

And yet…she was still frightened. Though she did not regret tonight, or any of the other nights, for that matter.

She should. But she didn't.

And that might have been the most dangerous thing of all.

ASH SHOULD NOT BE THINKING about her like this.

He should not be watching the delicate rise and fall of her bare chest, should not be marveling at the way she sighed in the aftermath of taking her pleasure, stretching like a satisfied cat in his arms.

He had never cared much for lingering after sex. Never cared much for talking to the women he slept with.

Yet here he was.

He couldn't stop looking at her.

She had blindsided him in ways he never expected. Yes, she was beautiful—achingly so. And yes, she had wit and sharpness and an ability to hold her own against anyone. But it wasn't just that.

It was the way she fought.

She had been cast out, ridiculed, treated as less than, and yet—she had not allowed it to break her.

And damn it all, Ash admired her.

And when, in all his life, had he ever *admired* a woman he was madly, achingly attracted to?

She was leaving England.

That news had hit him like a punch to the gut.

Logically, he understood it. She had every reason to go, every right to take back control of her own life. The same men who whispered about her behind their hands were no doubt indulging in far worse at this very moment in the private rooms of this very club. In fact, Marsden himself was often here. Ash had seen him more than once.

Clare was right. It wasn't bloody fair.

And yet.

Ever since she had spoken the words, *I'm leaving*, something inside him had shifted.

He had tried to tell himself that once she was gone, it would be for the best. That he had only wanted an affair, and now he had one. That she had been clear—she would return to the club to gamble, and while she was here, they could continue this arrangement.

But God help him, it would never be enough.

He would miss her.

And *he did not want her to go.*

Worse still—he had his suspicions about how she was earning her money. She had a knack for faro, yes, but he had heard whispers of a rigged roulette wheel. And after watching her win, again and again, at what should have been a pure game of chance… he no longer believed the rumors to be just rumors.

No doubt she had decided to take advantage of a world that had taken advantage of her.

And damn him, he couldn't blame her.

But the thing he truly couldn't wrap his head around? She had insisted—*no falling in love.*

Why had she even said it? *He* certainly hadn't been

thinking about love. Hell, he didn't even know what love was.

So why had she brought it up?

Unless…

No.

No, *that* was impossible.

She couldn't possibly think *she* was in danger of falling in love with *him*.

Could she?

The thought was absurd. Preposterous.

And yet, as he studied her, his body still thrumming with satisfaction, his mind a tangled mess of thoughts, he couldn't shake the feeling that he was missing something.

Then Clare looked at him.

And damn it all, there was naked desire in her gaze.

Whatever questions plagued him, whatever doubts he had—none of it mattered.

Not right now.

Right now, all that mattered was her.

He moved over her, caging her beneath him, capturing her mouth in a kiss that was both fierce and reverent. He threaded his fingers through hers, pinning her hands beside her head as he slid inside her, swallowing her moan as he filled her completely.

And for now, *this* was enough.

He would worry about everything else tomorrow.

CHAPTER TWENTY-SIX

The next time they met at the club, there was no discussion. It was as if they'd been drawn together by an unspoken pull that was impossible to resist. And just like before, it had ended in tangled sheets and breathless surrender. Words had been scarce, their bodies speaking first—only afterward, when the heat had settled, did conversation begin.

Ash held Clare close, their bodies still tangled in the aftermath of their passion. Her skin was warm against his, her breath slow and steady. He traced his fingers along the curve of her back, feeling the delicate rise and fall of her breaths. He should have been content, but a question burned inside him, one he could no longer silence.

"Why did you give yourself to him?" he asked, his voice barely above a whisper.

Clare stiffened slightly, and he felt her exhale against his chest. "Marsden?" She let out a breathless laugh, though there was no humor in it. "I've asked myself that same question a thousand times."

Ash turned his head, pressing a kiss to her temple. "You

must have known the risk. What would happen if you were wrong about him?"

"Oh, I knew." She tilted her head up to look at him, her eyes shadowed by something distant, something painful. "But it doesn't matter, does it? What's done is done."

"It matters to me." He tightened his arms around her. "I'd like to know."

She sighed, shifting onto her back and staring at the ceiling. "The short answer? Because of my mother."

Ash frowned. "I don't understand."

Clare let out a tired chuckle. "And I didn't either. Not back then. Not when I was eighteen and desperate. If only I could go back and tell that naïve, frightened girl a thing or two."

He watched as she chewed on her bottom lip, eyes lost in memory. "What would you tell her?" he whispered, running a slow, soothing hand along her hip.

She swallowed, her voice quieter now. "I'd tell her not to be so desperate to get away from Mama that she fell for the first person who showed her the slightest hint of affection."

Ash felt something tighten in his chest. The words hit too close, striking a part of him he had long buried. He would have done anything to escape his father, only his father hadn't cared what he did. He had only ever cared about his grandson, his grandson who would *never* be born.

"I suppose that sounds insane to you," Clare finished.

Ash shook his head, the ghosts of the past creeping in. "No," he said solemnly. "That doesn't sound insane to me at all."

Clare turned to him, brows lifting in question. "No?"

He gave a sad smile. "In fact, I understand all too well."

Her gaze searched his, curiosity obviously warring with something deeper. "How could you?"

He exhaled heavily, brushing a stray lock of hair from her

cheek. "Because I did the opposite. A thing I was only able to do because I'm a man. Instead of trying to escape into marriage, I escaped by refusing to commit to one."

Recognition flickered in Clare's eyes, the understanding settling between them like a quiet, unspoken truth. She nodded slowly. "We're not so different, are we?"

Ash traced the line of her jaw, the softness of her lips. "No. We aren't," he whispered.

She leaned into his touch, closing her eyes, and for the first time in years, he felt something shift inside him. A crack in the walls he had so carefully built.

He had spent so long running, hiding behind meaningless affairs and empty nights, believing love was nothing more than a trap. But here, in the dim glow of dawn, with Clare in his arms, he wondered if he had been wrong. If, perhaps, love wasn't the prison he had feared—but the key to setting him free.

CHAPTER TWENTY-SEVEN

Thursday night, The Duke of Southbury's Town House

Dinner was a disaster.

At least for Clare.

Meredith and Griffin chatted pleasantly, speaking of the latest theater performances and the coming holidays, as if nothing in the world was amiss. Meanwhile, beneath the table, Ash was ruining her.

She barely breathed as his fingers traced lazy circles on her thigh, the touch featherlight, maddening. He inched higher, closer, teasing, knowing exactly what he was doing to her.

And damn it, she wanted him there.

She wanted his hand to slip between her legs, to find her slick and aching. She wanted his fingers inside her, curling forward in that devastating way he had taught her could undo her completely.

But not here.

Not in the middle of *dinner*.

Not when Meredith and Griffin were sitting right across from them.

Her skin burned as she forced herself to reach for her glass, her fingers trembling slightly around the stem.

How had it come to this?

They regularly met at the Onyx Club. Again and again and again. She sneaked out at night after her hosts were asleep, hiring a hack at the corner to take her there. She had long since surpassed the amount of money she needed to escape and had more than enough tucked away to take her far from England.

So why was she still here?

Arranging travel should have been easy. A few discreet inquiries, a carriage to the coast, a ship across the Channel. She should have already done it.

But she hadn't.

Because of him.

Because she wanted *this*—his touch, his heat, his wicked mouth whispering the kind of things that made her toes curl. But worse, she wanted his company.

That was the most dangerous part.

He was more than just a lover. He was clever and charming, sharp in the way she liked. She had spent years feeling like an outcast, on the outside of every conversation, every gathering. But with him, she belonged.

And she didn't want to give that up.

Not yet.

Ash's fingers glanced off her inner thigh, and she sucked in a sharp breath, her grip tightening on her wine glass. The stem wobbled between her fingers, nearly toppling, and every glass on the table jumped.

Meredith placed a hand at her throat, startled. Griffin's hand caught the table's edge.

"Clare, dear, are you quite all right?" Meredith asked, concern in her voice.

Clare barely swallowed a curse. She grabbed her napkin, dabbing at her lips, hiding her shock behind it.

"I—I'm not feeling entirely well," she said quickly. "Excuse me, won't you?"

She pushed back from the table before she had to look at Ash. Because if she did, she knew exactly what she would see.

Mischief.

Triumph.

And something else she wasn't prepared to name.

She made it into the corridor, pressing her palms to the cool wall, inhaling deeply, steadying herself.

She knew he would come. It was only a matter of time.

And *he did*.

The door creaked open, and the moment he stepped into the hallway, she seized his wrist and pulled him into the darkened drawing room.

His lips were on hers in an instant.

He backed her against the door, his hands sliding into her hair, his mouth hot and insistent, taking, demanding. And *damn her*, she let him.

She let him because *this* was why she hadn't left. *This* was why she kept coming back.

Her fingers tangled in his hair, her body arching into him —until, with every last bit of willpower she had, she wrenched herself away.

"I must speak to you," she panted.

He was breathing just as heavily. "And I must *touch* you."

His lips found her neck, his voice low and hungry. "Feeling you in there was driving me insane."

Her eyes rolled back as his mouth brushed over the pulse behind her ear.

No. No, she had to say it.

"Ash," she forced out.

He kissed along her throat.

"Ash, I'm serious."

He didn't listen. He nipped lightly at the place just above her collarbone.

She shoved him away.

Hard.

And when she put the settee between them, only then did he exhale sharply, his hands going to his hips. "What is it you need to tell me that's so bloody important?"

She straightened her spine. Her hands curled into fists at her sides. "We must stop."

Silence.

"No more of this," she said, waving a finger in the air between them.

Ash went completely still.

"Why?" His voice was measured, but there was something else there. Frustration? Disappointment?

She swallowed. "Because I have the money. I have everything I need. And I must leave before my mother arrives."

He ran a hand through his hair, clearly agitated. "When will that be?"

She hesitated. "A sennight at most."

His jaw tensed. "Then we have a sennight."

"No," she said quickly, shaking her head. "No, you're not listening. We must stop *now*."

His gaze darkened. But his voice was softer when he asked, "You don't want me anymore?"

The ache in his eyes almost undid her.

She forced herself to turn away. "I cannot say that," she whispered.

"Then don't."

She felt him before she saw him—his presence closing in behind her, his breath at her ear.

How could she make him understand? Their time together had been unforgettable. But that was the problem. She was losing herself in him, in the feelings growing too fast, too strong. The more time they spent together, the more he bound her to him—his touch, his body, his intimate whispers pulling her deeper. Letting him go needed to be easy. It should have been.

But it wasn't.

They'd had their fun. More than enough. And this was no longer just about her reputation or the risk of scandal. Her heart was on the line now, and that was a risk she could no longer take.

"I've never wanted anyone the way I want you, Clare."

Her eyes squeezed shut. "I can't stay here and be your lover, Ash."

Those words *stopped him cold.*

And she could tell. *That* was when he realized.

Because for the first time since all of this began, he was truly asking her for something that wasn't in her best interest.

And he had clearly never thought about it that way before.

She exhaled, bracing herself. "I must leave."

He scrubbed a hand over his face, as if trying to clear his thoughts. "But…but…you have other options."

She let out a sharp, humorless laugh. "What options? I cannot be a nursemaid. I cannot be a lady's maid. Who would ever hire me? I can do *nothing* but listen to my mother's disappointment for the rest of my life."

"You *do* have options," he insisted, pacing away from her.

"Really?" she challenged. "Name one."

"You can marry me!"

CHAPTER TWENTY-EIGHT

At first, she laughed.

A real, full-bodied laugh, the kind he loved pulling from her, the kind that made her dark eyes glimmer with delighted amusement.

But then she realized *he wasn't laughing.*

Her laughter tapered off as she took him in—his tight jaw, his arms crossed over his chest, his stance too rigid.

His seriousness.

The humor in her gaze dimmed, but her lips still curved slightly, as if waiting for him to admit he was merely jesting. "You're not serious."

Ash *wasn't sure* he was serious.

Hell, he hadn't even been thinking when he said it. The words had just happened. But now that they were out there, now that he had seen the way her face had changed, the way her eyes had flickered with something unreadable before she masked it…

Now, he *was* serious.

He pushed off the mantel and exhaled sharply, running a hand through his hair. "I'm quite serious," he muttered, though even to his own ears, he sounded like a man still trying to convince himself.

Clare's lips twitched, as if she could hear the hesitation too. "Forgive me if I find that difficult to believe."

He rubbed the back of his neck roughly, because damn it all, he didn't know what the hell he was saying, just that he couldn't let her leave. "I admit, I'm not entirely certain where the idea came from—"

Clare snorted. "That much is clear."

"But now that I've said it," he went on, forcing himself to meet her gaze, "I am… serious."

Her head tilted, eyes narrowing with skepticism. "Serious, are you? With that hesitation in your voice?"

He grasped his lapel. "Clare, I would never—"

"You would never *seriously* propose," she finished for him, the humor draining from her tone, replaced by something firmer. A warning. "We've had fun. *A lot* of fun," she admitted, an unmistakable heat flickering in her eyes before she pushed it down. "But it's time to end this. Beyond time, if we're honest."

A sharp twist of something—something raw and unfamiliar—hit him square in the chest.

He scrubbed a frustrated hand through his hair. "Now who's not listening?"

She stepped closer then, too close, her palm coming to rest on his shoulder, warm and steady. A gentle squeeze. Comforting.

He hated it.

Because she was already saying good-bye.

"Let's not make this more difficult than it needs to be," she said, soft but firm. "We both knew from the start that this couldn't last forever. Didn't we?"

"Well, I—" *Bloody hell. This was excruciating.*

Because he didn't know what he knew any longer. Only

that the thought of her leaving—of her disappearing into France, living some fabricated life, of him never seeing her again—felt like someone was tying his gut into knots.

"Why *couldn't* we marry?" he demanded.

She groaned—*actually groaned*—and tilted her head toward the ceiling. "Oh, allow me to count the ways."

Then she *patted* him.

Patted.

Like he was some poor, misguided fool.

His teeth clenched.

"It's sweet of you to suggest it," she went on, shaking her head, smiling—but not the kind of smile he wanted to see. This one was sad, sympathetic, resigned. "Really. But you are not required to be my hero, Ash."

His breath caught. He wanted to growl.

"I shall go to France," she continued lightly. "Live my lovely life as a would-be widow. You shall forget all about me and move on to your next amusement—whoever she shall be."

Forget her?

Move on?

His chest tightened.

"You don't want to stay?" he asked roughly, his jaw tight. "Is that it?"

Clare let out a long, measured sigh. The kind of sigh one gives a petulant child who simply doesn't understand.

She turned for the door. And panic flared hot and sharp in his chest.

"I expect," she said over her shoulder, an annoyingly flippant edge to her voice, "that in the cold light of day, you'll regret ever having said this."

His hands curled into fists. "No, I shall not regret it!" he shot back, straightening. Damn it, he was digging in.

Clare sighed again, heavier this time, and opened the door. "Then you leave me no choice."

A sick feeling coiled in his gut.

"I am not going back to the Onyx Club," she said matter-of-factly. "And I shall not attend another one of these dinners."

His stomach dropped.

"I am making my arrangements," she finished, turning and looking him straight in the eye. "And I am leaving for France."

And then she was gone.

Ash stared after her, heart pounding, breath unsteady, hands shaking at his sides. His world had just been shaken.

And for the first time in his entire life, he had no idea what the hell to do.

CHAPTER TWENTY-NINE

Clare dipped the quill into the inkwell, then pressed it to the crisp vellum. The letter to the innkeeper along the shores of Calais had to be brief—just enough to confirm her arrival, nothing that could be traced back to her if someone got curious.

She'd heard about the place from one of the servants, made discreet inquiries, exchanged coin for whispered directions. She couldn't afford too many detailed plans—couldn't risk anyone catching wind of what she was about to do. Some things would have to fall into place as she went.

The mail coach out of London would be simple enough. Then more coaches to the coast, which would be easy enough. A berth on a ship heading to Calais—not a problem.

Her maid had agreed to come with her. Turns out *she* didn't enjoy living in near exile in the country under Mama's watchful gaze any more than Clare did.

Everything was in motion. Everything was almost done.

So why did she feel like she was coming apart at the seams?

She exhaled slowly, sealing the letter. Next, she wrote her good-byes.

One for Meredith—brief, apologetic, loving. A promise not to worry, though she knew her friend would. Meredith had a baby to think about. That had to come first. Clare just hoped, one day, after the child was born, that Meredith and Griffin might find their way to France for a visit. The thought was the only thing keeping her afloat at the moment.

Another letter for her mother—colder, more final, indicating that she would not return.

No doubt, once the initial shock wore off, Mama would be relieved. Keeping a ruined daughter under her roof had not been ideal. This way, Clare would be giving her mother her freedom as well. And wasn't *that* what everyone wanted?

She swallowed against the lump rising in her throat.

The hardest part—the part she hadn't yet been able to face—was the last letter.

To Ash.

She had tried. She had started it half a dozen times, but every time, the words felt wrong. Too formal, too detached, too ridiculous.

She'd scratched through every pathetic attempt, finally giving up and tossing the damned vellum into the fire.

She didn't particularly like how they had ended things, but there was nothing left to say. Nothing that wouldn't make leaving harder than it already was. No doubt by now, Ash had realized she had been right all along.

She had saved him from himself—from whatever strange, impulsive madness had made him offer marriage in the first place. He just didn't know it yet.

Oh, how she had wanted to believe him.

Her heart had clenched the moment he'd said it, his voice raw with something that had almost convinced her. But when she had pressed him, he had hesitated.

And hesitation was not enough.

Not for marriage.

Not for a lifetime.

If there was one thing she knew, it was that a forced proposal, a reluctant proposal, would ruin both of them in the end.

She had never wanted one from Marsden. And she couldn't—*wouldn't*—accept one from Ash either. *Especially* not from Ash.

A soft knock at the door made her jump.

Heart pounding, she shoved the letter she had just finished into the drawer of the writing desk, smoothing her hands down the front of her gown.

"Come in," she called, just as the door pushed open.

Meredith stepped inside, her brows drawn together in concern. "I came to check on you," she said carefully.

Clare forced a bright smile, one that felt like it might shatter at the edges. "What do you mean? I'm fine." She gave her head a little shake.

Even to her own ears, the words rang false.

Meredith's gaze sharpened. She stepped closer, watching her too closely.

"You haven't seemed yourself lately," Meredith said gently.

Clare turned away.

She didn't want Meredith to see the guilt on her face.

"Oh, perhaps I've been a bit tired," she deflected, standing and moving toward the bed, brushing an invisible wrinkle from the sheets. "But as I'm not the one carrying a babe, I'm loath to complain." She turned, forcing another too-bright smile.

Meredith rubbed her belly with a soft chuckle. "Oh, complain all you like," she teased. "Heaven knows I intend to."

Clare huffed a laugh—one that wasn't entirely real.

Meredith's smile faded slightly as she stepped back toward the door, but then she hesitated. "Are you certain there's nothing bothering you?" she asked. "Griffin and I both got the distinct impression that you and Ash had… words the other night."

Clare's stomach dropped.

Oh, no.

Of course Meredith had noticed.

It wasn't the first time she and Ash had left dinner at the same time—had disappeared into a dimly lit corridor or an empty room. Her friends weren't fools.

Clare swallowed hard, forcing her voice into something steady, if not entirely believable. "I'm fine. Truly."

No matter how much she might want to, she couldn't tell Meredith the truth. Couldn't tell her that she'd been sleeping with her brother, that she was leaving forever, that Ash had asked her to marry him, and she had refused. Meredith didn't deserve the burden of any of that news. Especially not in her condition.

Guilt clawed at Clare though. How would Meredith feel when she learned the truth? The part about her leaving, at least. Meredith would try to talk her out of it. Clare knew that much. It was another reason she'd decided not to share her plans.

Meredith sighed. "I expect you're not looking forward to going back to the countryside with your mother."

Clare let out a relieved breath. *A perfect excuse.*

"You're right," she said quickly, exhaling in a rush.

"Well, at least she said she won't fetch you until Sunday, which means you can still come with us to the Merriweathers' ball on Friday evening. You are still planning to attend, aren't you?" Meredith pressed, eyeing her carefully from the side.

Her friend had spent the better part of the last fortnight begging Clare to attend just one social event. She had finally capitulated, but she was hardly looking forward to it. Being gossiped about all evening was not something she relished.

"I'll go," Clare allowed, feeling entirely numb inside.

"Excellent." Meredith watched her closely for a moment longer, as if she still wasn't quite convinced. "You'd tell me, wouldn't you?" Meredith pressed. "If you *weren't* all right?"

God, the guilt was unbearable.

Clare nodded too quickly, too forcefully. "Yes, yes. Of course."

Meredith still looked doubtful, but she let it go. "Very well then. We'll see you at dinner?"

"Of course." Clare somehow managed another smile.

Meredith lingered for only a moment before slipping out the door. The second it clicked shut, Clare's entire body sagged.

She lowered herself to sit hard on the bed, her limbs boneless, heavy, exhausted.

She was the worst liar in the world.

And *Meredith knew it.*

Maybe she hadn't figured it out yet—maybe she wouldn't until it was too late—but deep down, Clare knew her friend could see right through her.

And that was almost as unbearable as the thought of leaving Ash behind.

CHAPTER THIRTY

Ash spent the morning riding through the park, but the crisp air did little to clear the chaos in his mind. He had woken up feeling like a man on the verge of something disastrous.

Clare had sent him away and refused to see him again. And instead of brushing it off, instead of moving on like he always did, he had barely slept. His thoughts were consumed with her—her laugh, her sharp wit, the way she fit against him as if she had been made just for him.

And that was the problem.

He wasn't supposed to feel like this. He wasn't supposed to *care*.

So what the hell was wrong with him?

By midday, he found himself in Southbury's study, scowling into a glass of brandy. Southbury leaned back in his chair, watching him with his usual infuriating calm. "You look like hell."

Ash tipped his head back and groaned. "I feel like hell."

Southbury lifted both brows. "Let me guess. This has something to do with a certain scandalous young lady?"

Ash cleared his throat and shifted in his seat. "I'm going to ask you something, Southbury. Something shocking. But I want you to react in your normal, steadfast manner and be *completely* honest with me."

Southbury looked slightly concerned, but he nodded. "Go on."

Ash let out his breath in a pent-up rush. "How did you know when you were in love?"

To his credit, Southbury didn't even blink. "Ah. So that's what this is about."

"Just answer the damn question," Ash grumbled.

Southbury exhaled, setting down his glass. He bit his lip and contemplated the question for a moment. "It wasn't one thing. It was everything. I couldn't get Meredith out of my head. I hated the thought of any other man having her. And, most of all, I knew my life would be *less* without her in it." He paused, then arched a brow. "Sound familiar?"

Ash ran a hand through his hair, his pulse hammering. *Shit. Shit. Shit.*

This was exactly what he felt for Clare.

The obsession. The possessiveness. The sheer, unrelenting need to have her in his life.

Southbury studied him for a long moment. "I know how difficult this is for you." His voice was slow and calm, without a trace of pity—thank God.

Ash swallowed. Hard. Southbury had known his father. That's what he was talking about. But Ash did *not* want to talk about his father. Not now. Not *ever*. "*Don't—*"

"Your father always said love was a weakness. That's why you've been fighting it, isn't it?"

Ash stiffened. "This has *nothing* to do with him."

. . .

"DOESN'T IT?" Southbury's voice was quiet but firm. "That and your long-standing declaration that you'll never marry? Never produce an heir?"

A growl issued from Ash's throat. "I'm warning you, Southbu—"

"Your father treated love as if it were a cage, something to be avoided at all costs. And you—well, you've made damn sure to follow in his footsteps. Haven't you?"

Blood pounded in Ash's head. He'd never been one for violence outside of a boxing saloon, but at the moment, he wanted to smash his fist into Southbury's middle.

"I don't know what you said to him on his deathbed, Trentham," Southbury continued. "But I suspect it had something to do with informing him that he'd never be a grandfather."

A muscle ticked in Ash's jaw. His nostrils flared. His mind raced back. It had been years ago. But he still remembered it like it was yesterday.

He'd walked into his father's sickroom, the giant bedchamber at his country estate. A place Father rarely visited in all the years since Mama died during Meredith's birth. A place he'd left his two young children to be cared for exclusively by servants. A place where—when he had deigned to visit—he did nothing but berate and belittle his only son.

Ash had long since shut away any trace of emotion he might have felt for his father. To him, the man was nothing short of a monster. He had sold Meredith into marriage with a decrepit old lecher and had never once shown the slightest interest in Ash or his life. His father cared for no one but himself. And the only reason Ash had come to see him one final time was for a singular purpose.

~

ASH HADN'T WANTED *to see him again. He honestly didn't care if Father died alone. But Meredith was there, of course, sitting in a chair next to their father, crying. She'd looked up at him with red-rimmed eyes, nodding when he'd asked to speak with the old man alone. She'd stood and hurried from the room, leaving Lord Harlowe Drake, the Marquess of Trentham, alone with his only son.*

Ash had stepped forward calmly, a calculated look of indifference on his face. The old man was withered, wasted away. He still possessed the same storm-gray eyes that both of his children had inherited, but other than the eyes, there was little else resembling the healthy man he'd once been.

"You came," Father croaked, reaching out a withered hand toward Ash.

"Indeed," was his stoic reply.

His father tried to push himself up on his pillows but, too weak with the fever that ailed him, he failed, and Ash would not assist him.

"I want you to promise me," Father said, coughing piteously.

Ash arched a brow. "Promise you what?"

More coughing ensued. "I want you to promise me that you'll take a bride. You'll marry and produce my grandson. You never saw fit to do so while I was healthy, but now that I'm—"

"Make no mistake," Ash had bitten out, his jaw tightly clenched. "I am not *here to say good-bye. And I'm* not *here to make you any promises, save one."*

His father's wrinkled brow had wrinkled further. His breath came in labored gasps. "Why are you here then, Ashford?" he managed.

Ash had taken great pleasure in leaning down, getting close enough to his father's ear so the old man would be certain to hear every word. "My promise to you is that I will do no *such thing. I just came from the King's court, where I informed everyone present that I have absolutely no intention of either marrying or fathering an heir. The Trentham title will die with me."*

A look of horror came across his father's decrepit face. It was a look Ash would never forget. A look he took pleasure in.

"You cannot be serious," Father rasped before another coughing fit overtook him.

Ash allowed a slow, smug smile to spread across his face. "Oh, I'm serious. Entirely so. You spent your life ignoring Meredith and me, using us when it served your purposes, treating us like possessions."

"But I... I..."

"Do you realize, Father, the only time you ever contacted me since I've been an adult was to ask me when I intended to marry?"

"That's not true." Father tried to sit up again. "There have been other times. After Meredith married. We met in my study in London. We spoke about—"

"We spoke about how you auctioned off your only daughter to a disgusting old man to pay a gambling debt," Ash told him. "And the only reason Meredith remains by your side now is because I could never break her heart and tell her the truth about you. She actually sees some good in you. But I am not under the same illusion. I see you for what you are. I always have."

"You would forego your duty, just to spite me?" Father asked, a snarl on his lips, his thin chest rising and falling with obvious anger.

"Oh, I'd do more than that, just to spite you." Ash straightened himself to his full height and tugged on the ends of his coat. "You ordered me about when I was a child, but I've long since stopped caring about anything you have to say. There will be no Trentham heir. And you can rot in hell."

And, his nostrils flaring with distaste, Ash had turned on his heel and walked away. There was nothing left to say.

❧

ASH SHOOK HIS HEAD, forcing himself to stop reliving that hated memory. "You're right," he said to Southbury. "I did promise him he'd never be a grandfather that day."

Southbury nodded sagely. "And all these years, it's been an easy promise for you to keep…because *you've never been in love*." Southbury paused a moment. No doubt for dramatic effect. "*Until now*."

Ash clenched his hands into fists.

But his friend wasn't finished.

"And now that you've fallen in love, you're questioning all of it. And I'm here to tell you that you should question it. No man remains the same throughout his life, Trentham. We all change over time, and if we're fortunate, we become the wiser for it."

Ash didn't answer. He let his friend's words settle like so many small anchors in his mind.

"And I *won't* remind you that you once told me that if you were ever so 'unfortunate' as to fall in love, you'd come right out and tell the lady your feelings." Southbury cleared his throat. "I believe you said you'd much rather be rejected than subject yourself to years of torment the way I did."

Ash couldn't help his smile. "Oh, you're *not* going to remind me of that, are you?"

Southbury gave him an unrepentant grin. "Hmm. I suppose it's too late now. But I must say, you were right. I should have told Meredith I loved her a hundred times before I ever did. I advise you not to make the same mistake."

Ash growled in the back of his throat. He wanted to argue with his friend. He wanted to tell him to go straight to hell. But he couldn't… Because—*damn him*—Southbury was right.

For years, Ash had convinced himself that love was something to be avoided, something that would trap him, control him, *ruin* him.

But sitting here now, the realization crashed over him like a tidal wave, and he understood the truth.

Love wasn't a weakness.

Love was Clare.

And, *God help him*, there was every indication that he was in love with her.

CHAPTER THIRTY-ONE

By the time he left Southbury's house, Ash was on a mission. He spent the rest of the day in his club's library, pulling out every book of poetry he could find, searching the pages for answers. But all he discovered were words that made his chest tighten—words about longing, about devotion, about wanting to be better for someone else.

Love? Was it this relentless force that made him feel as if he was losing his mind? As if he couldn't breathe when Clare wasn't near him? As if he didn't want to be in a world where she wasn't by his side?

He'd spent years watching his friends succumb to love, one after another, secure in the knowledge that it wasn't an emotion *he* was even capable of. He'd grown up in a house without a mother, without a father, with only Meredith as family. And, yes, of course, he would do anything for his sister, but this was different. This feeling eclipsed anything he'd ever encountered before. It was maddening. It was all-consuming. It was life-altering.

The books weren't any help. He tossed them aside and

scrubbed a hand through his hair. Next, he did the only thing he could think to…

He went to visit Lucian.

Lucian was even more calm and composed than Southbury. And while Southbury had fallen in love with Meredith when they were still children, Lucian had taken his time realizing his feelings for Gemma. In fact, the man had married her after being forced to due to a scandal and then proceeded to leave the country for *over a year* while his new wife remained in London alone. Hardly the proper way to go about a marriage.

When he'd finally returned, Gemma had demanded a divorce, and Lucian had finally had to realize what a mistake he'd made in not treating her like the prize she was from the start.

In short, Lucian had been a full-grown man when love had come his way, and he'd bungled the thing unmercifully at first. He'd even asked Ash for lessons in being charming. At the time, Ash had found it quaint that the stoic Duke of Grovemont had come to him looking for advice on matters of the heart.

Ash knew how to treat a woman, so it made a certain amount of sense. He did not, however, know how to *love* a woman, *or* how to convince a woman that he loved her. It was time for Grovemont to return the favor.

"Tell me what love feels like," Ash demanded as he threw himself into a chair across from his friend in Grovemont's study.

Lucian barely looked up from his ledgers. "Why?"

"Just answer the damned question." Blast. His friends weren't making this whole thing any easier for him.

Lucian sighed, setting down his quill. "It's terrifying," he said succinctly, making Ash's stomach lurch.

Grovemont met his gaze and continued with a shrug.

"Honestly, it's the realization that someone else has the power to wreck you. It's knowing that your happiness, your peace, your entire existence, is now tied to another person." He paused and arched a brow. "And the worst part? You wouldn't change it for anything."

Ash stared at him. Then he gulped.

Lucian smirked and crossed his arms over his chest. "Let me guess. You're in love."

Ash groaned, rubbing a hand down his face. "Damn it. I think I am."

Lucian chuckled, the hint of a smile tugging at his lips. "Took you long enough."

≈

BY NIGHTFALL, Ash had a plan.

By all accounts, it seemed to him that he was most certainly in love. It was surprising, it was alarming, but it was true. Love, it seemed, didn't wait for an invitation, rather, it sneaked up on a man when he least suspected it.

He had to accept that by telling Clare he loved her and asking for her hand, he would be letting go of the promise he'd made at his father's deathbed. But Southbury had been right—a man wasn't meant to stay the same forever. He should grow, change, and gain wisdom along the way. Clinging to the anger of his past would be nothing short of foolish. He would not spite himself by spiting a dead man. He would not allow his father to have that power from the grave.

Besides, it wasn't as if he had a choice anymore. As Grovemont had said, once you fell in love, you wouldn't change it for anything. And Ash knew, with absolute certainty, that he didn't want a life without Clare in it. And he suspected—no, *prayed*—that she felt the same.

As for Clare's reputation, he didn't give a toss. Let the gossips gossip. He only knew one thing for certain: he wanted her as his marchioness. And if she wanted him too, that was all that mattered.

For a moment, he considered consulting his sister. But Meredith was a hopeless secret keeper—everyone knew that. If he confided in her that he was wildly in love with her closest friend and on the verge of making an offer, she'd likely ruin his entire plan.

No, best to let Mere be surprised. He doubted she'd object after she learned the truth. After all, she'd been trying to marry him off for ages. Well, she was about to get her wish. *With any luck*. He smiled to himself, already picturing her reaction.

But first, he had to convince Clare. Convince her that he loved her and that he truly wanted to marry her. Only then would she give him an honest answer about whether she felt the same. He suspected she hadn't taken him seriously before because he hadn't been certain enough himself. That would change. The next time, he would leave no room for doubt.

Of course, Clare—stubborn, impossible woman that she was—wouldn't make it easy for him. She would fight him. He knew it.

At the moment, she wouldn't even see him.

Which meant he had to outmaneuver her.

CHAPTER THIRTY-TWO

Thursday, The Duke of Southbury's Town House

Clare folded her arms over her chest and stared at Ash, one brow arched high in blatant skepticism.

A fire.

Really?

How convenient.

She wasn't certain what was more absurd—the fact that he expected them to believe such an obvious fabrication or the way he delivered the news with that casual, almost bored indifference, as if it were the most natural thing in the world for him to show up unannounced, bags in hand, ready to settle in at his sister's town house like an invited guest.

Griffin, ever the gracious host, merely sighed and signaled for the butler to see to Ash's accommodations.

Meredith, however, wasn't buying it for a second.

"A fire?" she repeated, her skeptical gaze narrowing on her brother. "Where exactly?"

Ash waved a vague, dismissive hand. "Kitchen. Nothing serious."

Griffin frowned. "You have a cook, don't you?"

"Yes," Ash said smoothly, already shrugging out of his coat, "but she wasn't the one setting things aflame this time."

Clare caught the flicker of his gaze in her direction, the barest hint of a smile playing at his lips.

Her pulse kicked up.

The *audacity* of this man.

She didn't believe him. Not for a second. She just hadn't worked out what his game was yet. Still, she held her tongue. *For now.*

The four of them settled in for a game of whist in the drawing room, and if Meredith or Griffin noticed the thinly veiled innuendo laced through Clare and Ash's banter, they wisely chose to ignore it.

"You do realize," Clare said dryly, as Ash laid down a particularly ruthless card, "that being insufferable is not, in fact, a requirement to win."

"Ah, but it makes victory all the sweeter," Ash murmured, his eyes gleaming with mischief.

She rolled her eyes, but her lips twitched before she could stop them.

The game went on, but soon, predictably, the conversation took a turn.

Meredith, ever eager to see her brother settled, wasted no time pressing the one topic Ash always sidestepped.

"Any closer to finding a wife, Brother?" she asked, taking a delicate sip of her wine.

Clare, as always, expected him to dodge. To smirk and offer some halfhearted deflection.

Instead, Ash answered immediately. "Yes, actually. I've already made my choice. I can only hope the lady in question says yes."

Clare choked on her wine. She gasped and coughed, slapping at her chest. *Did he truly just say that?*

Griffin gave them both *a look*. Oh, God. What did *he* know about it?

Meredith blinked at her brother slowly, giving him a perfectly skeptical glare. "You needn't make fun," she said, lifting her nose in the air and tossing a card upon the table.

"I'm not," Ash countered smoothly, completely unfazed. "I've given it quite a lot of thought lately, and I've decided you're right. It's high time I take a wife."

Clare stared at him, her mind scrambling to make sense of this unexpected turn of events.

What.

Was.

He.

Doing?

"Oh, really," Meredith drawled, clearly not believing a word of it. "Then, do tell, who is this woman? She must be a paragon if you've decided to ask for her hand."

Ash shook his head. "Ah, I cannot reveal her name until I have secured the lady's hand. But she is indeed someone quite special."

"You won't share her name?" Meredith retorted, obviously miffed. "Why not?"

"She may refuse me," Ash replied, blinking piteously toward Clare.

What was he about? Clare tugged at the neck of her gown. It was blistering hot in the drawing room of a sudden. She narrowed her eyes. "I seem to recall you once saying you wanted a *biddable* wife."

"I wouldn't object," Ash said far too quickly and far too agreeably.

"Oh, so a broodmare then?" she shot back. "You'd have better luck searching the stables."

Ash turned his gaze on her, something sharp and

knowing in his expression. "Well," he said smoothly, "I do like a spirited filly."

Heat bloomed in Clare's chest.

Not because of *what* he said. But because of *how* he said it.

Low.

Silky smooth.

Possessive.

The kind of voice that made promises. The kind of voice that— *No.*

Absolutely not.

She swallowed hard and forced herself to roll her eyes, refusing to let him see how that single sentence had affected her.

But suspicion prickled at the back of her mind. What was he doing here? Why had he suddenly arrived at his sister's home, talking about wanting a wife?

And why—*why*—was *her* name flashing through her mind as the *only* possible answer?

She refused to entertain the thought.

Refused.

Mercifully, Meredith chose that moment to yawn, stretching languidly as she set her cards down. "Well, that's enough excitement for me," she declared. "I'm off to bed."

Griffin followed suit, tossing his cards down as well. "Me too."

Clare began to rise, eager to escape with her friends, but Meredith stopped her with a knowing smile. "Stay and have a drink with Ash," she said lightly. "It's fine. We aren't formal here. Perhaps he'll tell *you* who he plans to ask to marry him."

"I just might!" Ash nearly shouted from his seat at the card table.

Clare froze, glancing at him. He looked far too pleased with himself. Her suspicion deepened.

This was a trap.

She should *leave.*

She *knew* she should.

Instead, she sighed and settled back into her chair, reaching for her glass.

CHAPTER THIRTY-THREE

The moment the door closed behind Meredith and Southbury, Ash poured Clare a much stronger drink than the wine she had been sipping.

She accepted it with obvious wary suspicion.

"Why do I have a feeling your house is not actually on fire?" she asked, narrowing her eyes over the rim of her glass.

Ash shrugged, swirling the amber liquid in his own glass. "That obvious, am I?"

"Yes." She gave her head that little shake he'd come to covet.

"Well," he said, taking a measured sip, "what choice did I have when you refused to see me?"

Clare let out a slow breath, setting her drink down on the table in front of her with deliberate care. "I refused to see you for good reason."

He inclined his head. "And that reason was?"

She lifted her chin. "Because I need to leave. And because I can't do *this*." She rolled a finger in the air.

Ash ignored the sharp pang in his chest. "I don't want you to leave," he said quietly.

"You don't—" She sucked in her breath.

His gaze captured hers and held. "I need time to convince you to marry me."

Clare froze. For a long moment, she didn't breathe. Then…

"What?" she said flatly. "Have you lost your mind?" But she could hear it, the inflection in her own voice, the tremor, the emotion she hadn't wanted to escape.

"I have not lost my mind," Ash said firmly. "In fact, I've done quite a lot of research on the matter."

Clare made a strangled sound in the back of her throat. "Research."

"Yes. I've made a study of it." He exhaled, running a hand through his hair. "In addition to speaking to Southbury and Grovemont, I—"

Her head snapped up, panic gripping her heart. "Griffin knows about this?"

"Yes, well, he had to help me identify it. I suspect it's why he and my sister were so quick to leave an unmarried couple alone in their drawing room."

Clare's eyes widened. "Identify what?"

Ash waved a hand. "I'm getting to that. As I was saying…I spoke to Southbury and Grovemont, and I went to the library and read scads of poems about love."

Clare gasped. *Love?*

Ash had to bite back a smile at the genuine horror on her face.

"Poems," she repeated, slowly, as if making sense of his words. "Poems about *love?*"

He nodded. "Turns out love is a terribly unique feeling. I'd never felt it before, so I didn't recognize it at first. You can't blame me, really."

Clare gaped at him. "Now you're beginning to frighten me."

Ash set his glass down and watched her carefully. "Will you stay and give me time to convince you to marry me?"

Clare had begun shaking her head even before he finished his sentence. "No. *No.* I'm leaving Saturday."

Ash sighed. "I expected you'd say that." He leaned back in his chair and steepled his fingers together, contemplating her with narrowed eyes. "And I've been thinking quite a bit about your plan to leave England."

Clare tensed. "What about it?" she asked, her eyes filled with suspicion.

"You said you'd write to Meredith once you arrived in France. To let her know you're fine."

She touched a hand to her throat. "Yes."

Ash inclined his head. "But what if you're *not* fine?"

She frowned. "Why wouldn't I be?"

Because I won't be there.

He didn't say it. Instead, he let the words linger between them.

"All sorts of horrors can befall a woman alone," he said instead.

Clare let out a long, exasperated sigh. "Oh, thank you *so very much* for pointing that out. I'm quite well aware. I'll have my maid with me, at least."

Ash met her gaze. Damn. She wasn't budging. He would have to try another tactic. "If you won't stay, let me come with you then."

The words shocked even him. But if she refused to stay, he would have to go. It was as simple as that.

Clare went still. Her eyes narrowed. "With me where?"

"To France, of course."

She stood up so fast her chair nearly toppled over. Then she backed away. "Right," she muttered. "I'm going to ring for a servant to come and fetch you now, because you've *clearly* got some sort of fever."

Ash stood and made it to her side in two strides. "Nothing of the sort," he murmured, leaning down and whispering the words next to her delicate ear.

She swallowed, pressing both hands to her middle. "You know this is madness."

"Delirious, reckless madness," he agreed, his voice low, rough. "And yet, here we are."

He pressed his nose to her jaw, inhaling the scent of her. The scent he had come to crave. "I have just one question for you."

"W…what?" Her breath hitched.

Ash smiled to himself. She may not be ready to admit she loved him, but she still wanted him. He could tell by the way her body tensed, the way she shivered at his touch. His fingers brushed down the side of her arm, slow, teasing. "Do you want me?"

She blinked, clearly caught off guard. "What?" Her voice was a ragged whisper.

He pressed forward, close enough to feel the heat of her body. This was a gamble. A calculated risk. Perhaps it wasn't fair to use his body and his voice to seduce her, but he wasn't in the mood to be fair. He had to show her that what they had between them was real…and rare. But yes, it was a gamble. And if she ran now, he would be lost.

But she didn't run.

"Do you want me?" he repeated, his voice a rasp against her ear.

"Ash, I—" Her throat worked as she swallowed.

"Answer the question, Clare," he whispered, tilting her chin up to meet his gaze. "Because if you say yes, I'm going to kiss you."

Her pulse fluttered beneath his fingertips. Silence stretched between them, thick and charged. Then, on a breathless exhale…

"Kiss me."

He didn't need any further encouragement.

He pulled her sharply into his arms, his lips crushing against hers, swallowing the soft gasp that escaped her throat.

Her hands found his hair, fingers twisting, tugging just enough to make him groan. He lifted her effortlessly, setting her on the edge of the table behind them.

She gasped as the cool wood met her bare thighs, her skirts already gathered in his impatient hands.

"We can't," she breathed, glancing toward the door, but her grip on him tightened. She was obviously worried about the fact that they were in an unlocked room.

"We already are," he said, trailing his fingers along the lace of her stockings, up, up, up.

And she didn't stop him.

Because when he kissed her again—hungry, possessive, consuming—there was no more room for logic. No more room for indecision.

Only pleasure.

Clare tiptoed to the door, her breath caught somewhere between her ribs. The household was still asleep. Even Ash had finally relented, allowing himself to be convinced that the "proper" thing to do was to return to his guest room—after he had stolen into hers and they had made love again.

The thought of it sent a shiver through her, though she refused to name the emotion stirring in her chest. It wasn't longing. It couldn't be.

She needed to leave. And the sooner the better. She'd plan to leave on Saturday, after attending the Merriweathers' ball with Meredith, before her mother arrived. But she knew now that she could not spend another night beneath the same roof as Ash. Not when his words from last night still echoed in her mind, a dangerous whisper against her heart.

He had spoken like a madman. Like a man on the verge of something foolish.

Like a man who might be in love.

No. *No.* He *wasn't* in love. He was confusing it with lust.

"I need time to convince you to marry me," he'd said. The

words had tumbled from his lips like dice upon a gaming table. Effortless, perhaps, but with high stakes. *Such* high stakes.

And for a moment last night, she'd considered it. Considered believing him. Considered pretending that he really was in love with her and wanted to marry her. But now that her blood had cooled, and she'd had time to think, she realized that had just been her foolish, traitorous heart wishing for things that could never be.

Ash kept insisting he wanted to marry her, but that was guilt talking, not love. A misplaced sense of honor, of duty. He wasn't finished with their affair. That was all. He didn't want her to leave—*yet*.

But the day would come, sooner rather than later, when he would wish her gone. Men like Ash weren't the marrying sort. And she—she refused to be left. Not again.

Her grip tightened around her valise, fingers pressing hard into the soft leather as she stepped toward the door of her bedchamber. She hesitated, her pulse loud in her ears.

The moment the door clicked shut behind her, she let out a slow, measured breath. One step down. Thousands more to go.

She moved quietly down the staircase, her movements swift but careful, her gaze darting around the dimly lit hall to ensure no one witnessed her flight. Shadows stretched long against the walls, distorted by the flickering sconces. It felt as if the house itself were watching her.

A hundred thoughts rushed through her mind at once, tumbling over each other like cards being shuffled. *Would* she be safe on the journey? Would she find a home—a life—in France?

And the most terrifying question of all: Was she doing the right thing?

She was. Wasn't she?

Her lips parted on a silent exhale, but the knot in her stomach only tightened. It wasn't the sex with Ash that had been a mistake. No, she would never regret that. His touch, his heat, the way he made her feel, the pleasure he'd given her—those were memories she would carry with her, locked away where no one could steal them.

The mistake was something else entirely.

The mistake was this feeling.

The way her heart clenched at the thought of never seeing him again.

The way she suddenly realized that, somewhere between scandal and secrecy, between teasing banter and whispered confessions in the dark, she had started to *care*.

And that? *That* was unacceptable.

She needed to get away from him, stay away from him. Before she did something truly, utterly foolish—like *fall in love with him*.

Determination hardened inside her, quiet but fierce. She reached the front door and curled her fingers around the handle. She'd left a note for her maid, asking her to meet her at the coaching station later this morning. For now, Clare needed to get out of this house.

Freedom was right beyond this portal. She could feel it. Nearly taste it.

She ripped open the door and took a sharp step back, her breath freezing in her throat.

For standing on the top step, her expression unreadable beneath the dim glow of dawn, was none other than...*her mother*.

CHAPTER THIRTY-FIVE

Clare sat curled in the corner of the settee, a book open in her lap, though she hadn't turned a single page in over twenty minutes. The words blurred together, unread and unabsorbed, her mind too preoccupied with the events of the morning.

Her mother's unexpected arrival had upended everything. She had been so close. So agonizingly close.

This morning, when she'd stepped onto the doorstep, valise in hand, her heart pounding with the thrill of escape, she had felt freedom at her fingertips. And then—there she stood. Her mother. A force of nature in lace-trimmed traveling attire, looking down at Clare with that razor-sharp gaze of hers, suspicion nipping at the edges of her perfectly controlled expression.

Clare had fumbled for an explanation, but before she could form the words, the butler had arrived, his presence a temporary reprieve from Mama's scrutiny. Then Meredith and Griffin had come down, bright and cheerful, welcoming their new house guest with warmth and ease, while Clare had seized the opportunity to slip away.

Back in her room, she had shoved the letters she'd left out into the depths of her drawer, pressed the valise to the farthest corner of her wardrobe, and locked away any lingering hope of escape.

She had waited too long.

And, infuriatingly, her mother had arrived too early.

The timing had been cruelly perfect. Clare had written to Mama last week, assuming she would arrive *after* the Merriweathers' ball as planned. The ball that was scheduled for tonight.

Her mother, of course, had made quite the show of insisting that she and Clare stay in and rest. That a ball was frivolous, unnecessary. They would return to the countryside in the morning, away from prying eyes and whispered conversations.

Clare hadn't argued. What did it matter? The only thing that had mattered—her escape—had been stolen from her.

But Meredith had been persuasive, as always. And eventually, Mama had relented, agreeing to allow Meredith and Griffin to escort Clare to the ball tonight.

"I hate to be the object of gossip," her mother had said pointedly, the words laced with sharp-edged disapproval. Clearly indicating that Clare was the one responsible for the whispers. That she was the one who ought to be ashamed.

Clare had said nothing. She didn't care whether she went to the ball. What difference did it make? She had lost her chance. The reality of her failure settled in her chest like lead.

She had been so close—so close to leaving this life behind, to disappearing before Ash could convince her to stay, before her mother could dictate her future, before Society could finish writing her story for her. And yet, she'd failed.

And she knew precisely why.

Her fingers curled tightly around the edges of her book.

It was Ash.

She'd been loath to leave Ash. So she had lingered too long. Held onto something that was never meant to last.

Now, she would have to wait until spring. There was no sneaking out of the country in the dead of winter. The servants there were all terrible gossips, and Clare had no doubt they would report any unusual behavior back to Mama. Not to mention the mail coachman would recognize her in an instant and ruin *any* attempt at secrecy.

No. London was her only hope of escape. And after tonight, she wouldn't be allowed to return until spring for her annual shopping trip with Mama.

At least Ash didn't know what she had tried to do this morning. That she had planned to disappear without a word, to leave him behind without so much as a good-bye. He'd tried more than once to get her alone to talk today, but he soon learned how closely her mother watched her during waking hours.

Clare exhaled slowly, closing her book.

The only amusing part of the day had been watching Ash interact with Mama.

Clare was used to people fawning over her mother. To watching them bow and scrape, treating Mama as if she were some long-suffering saint, the most tragically put-upon mother in the entire *ton*. She relished it, thrived on it, played the part of the martyr so well that even Clare, at times, almost believed it.

Meredith was one of the few who refused to indulge her, and today, Ash had done the same.

It had been unexpected. Startling, even. He had watched her mother with the same quiet calculation that Clare had come to know so well, but instead of playing along, instead of offering sympathies or praise, he had treated Mama as if *she* were the one who ought to be ashamed.

~

Luncheon had been a brittle affair. Clare sat rigidly beside her mother, Meredith and Griffin occupying either end of the table, while Ash sat directly across from the two ladies.

Clare maintained a carefully impassive expression while Meredith, ever gracious, attempted to draw her mother into conversation. Ash, meanwhile, seemed wholly uninterested in the soup, the silver, or the strained pleasantries—his attention remained fixed on Clare. She did not dare meet his gaze.

"We're enjoying such seasonable weather this year," Meredith offered with a hopeful smile.

"Indeed," Griffin replied, eager to assist.

"I only hope it holds until we return to the country," Clare's mother said coolly, lifting her spoon with delicate precision.

"You prefer the country, then?" Griffin asked politely.

A pause.

"Hardly," her mother replied. "But some households are compelled to retreat from Town when certain daughters have rendered London… less welcoming."

Griffin looked as though he might choke on his wine. Clare's face burned.

Ash's voice cut through the silence, smooth and measured. "One might say such misfortunes reflect less upon the daughter, and more upon those tasked with her care."

Clare's head snapped up. Had he truly just said that? No one spoke to Mama like that. Ever.

Her mother set her spoon down with quiet precision. "Are you suggesting I lacked vigilance, Lord Trentham?"

Ash offered a faint, unreadable smile. "Only that it's unfortunate when a young woman's brilliance goes unnoticed by those closest to her."

Her mother's chin lifted. "And yet, some things like impropriety are impossible to conceal—no matter how charming the packaging."

"Perhaps," Ash said lightly. "But some observers are clever enough to recognize a true gem, even when others prefer to overlook it."

A pause stretched, taut as piano wire.

Mama, for once, had no ready retort.

The moment was brief. But in it, something shifted.

Clare looked at Ash fully for the first time that afternoon, her breath catching at the quiet resolve in his gaze. He hadn't raised his voice, hadn't spoken out of turn—and yet he had done what no one else ever had.

He had stood up for her. Calmly. Without apology.

Her mother turned her attention back to her soup, the matter, for now, dismissed.

But Clare could scarcely taste a bite. The sting of humiliation still lingered—but beneath it, something warmer remained.

She lowered her eyes again, not out of shame, but to steady herself. Her heart, it seemed, was no longer entirely her own.

AND SO IT had continued throughout the day. Later, when Mama had made another biting comment—something else designed to remind Clare of her place—Ash had silenced her with a look. A single, deliberate look that carried more weight than words ever could.

Her mother had begun to watch him with unveiled disdain.

It was the most gratifying moment Clare had enjoyed in years while in her mother's presence.

By seven o'clock that evening, Mama had withdrawn to her guest room, complaining of a megrim, while Clare sat at her dressing table, gazing at her reflection, desperately searching for a reason to forgo the Merriweathers' ball.

She could picture it already. The glances, the whispers. Ash, standing across the ballroom, living the life he was meant for, while she was expected to fade into the background. To disappear, as if she had never existed at all.

She would be perfectly content to stay in. To remain hidden, safe from prying eyes and disapproving stares.

Then Meredith appeared in the doorway, arms crossed, expression set in unmistakable determination. "You're not ready?" she asked, giving Clare a once-over.

Clare didn't even look up. "I'm not going."

"Yes, you are."

She sighed. "Meredith—"

"You cannot keep hiding forever," her friend interrupted, stepping farther into the room.

"I'm *not* hiding."

Meredith arched a single, unimpressed brow.

Clare exhaled sharply, setting down her hairbrush with a quiet thud. "I simply don't enjoy these gatherings."

"Come on, Clare. You haven't been out socially in weeks." She placed on a hand on her belly. "And this is the last time *I'll* be able to go out in Society for months."

"I haven't been out socially in *years*," Clare muttered. "And I've survived just fine."

Meredith rolled her eyes. "You used to love parties. And you cannot let them win."

Clare stiffened. "Let who win?"

"The ones who whisper behind their fans. The ones who think you're too ashamed to show your face." Meredith met her gaze, steady and unyielding. "You aren't ashamed, are you?"

Clare narrowed her eyes. "Of course not."

"Then come," Meredith pressed. "Let them see you. Besides, this is your last taste of freedom before the winter."

Clare hesitated. Her friend knew her well, knew which argument to use to convince her. And normally, she would refuse. She would let them all go without her, content in the quiet solitude of her room.

But tonight… Tonight, something shifted.

Perhaps it was Meredith's words, the reminder that she had spent too long letting Society control her. Perhaps it was the anticipation of Ash's absence, the emptiness that was already settling in her chest at the thought of not seeing him again after she returned to the country tomorrow.

Or perhaps, just perhaps, she was tired of being the woman everyone whispered about.

Lifting her chin, she met Meredith's gaze. "Fine. I'll go."

A bright smile covered Meredith's face. "Good. Let's make them remember who you are."

And for the first time in a long time, Clare intended to do exactly that.

CHAPTER THIRTY-SIX

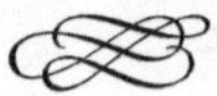

Ashford Drake was not a man who got nervous. He had faced duels, scandal, and enough would-be marchionesses to fill a ballroom. He had bluffed his way through high-stakes card games, talked his way out of sticky situations, and charmed his way into women's beds with nothing but a grin and a well-placed whisper.

But tonight?

Tonight, he was sweating through his cravat and felt like he might be violently ill.

Because tonight, he was going to ask Clare Handleton to marry him. Only this time, he intended to do it correctly, romantically, properly. This time would involve a ring and dropping to one knee, and the absolute certainty he wanted her to say yes.

The thought sent a rush of nerves straight through him, and he exhaled sharply, adjusting the cuffs of his jacket as he entered the grand ballroom. The chandeliers glittered overhead, and the air was thick with perfume and whispered gossip. He barely registered any of it.

His eyes found her instantly.

Clare.

She stood across the room, poised and radiant in that glowing ember gown he remembered from the house party, the one that made her golden hair shine like the last bit of light at sunset. The candlelight caught in her profile, making it glow, and when she turned slightly, he caught the sharp, intelligent gleam in her dark eyes—the same gleam that had always made him want to chase her, to challenge her, to *keep* her.

And now? Now, he was about to irreversibly change himself for her.

And he couldn't wait. He was eager for it.

He strode toward her without hesitation, ignoring the murmurs that followed him as he cut through the crowd. By the time she noticed him, it was too late to escape.

"Dance with me," he said, holding out his hand.

A flicker of something unreadable crossed her face, but she didn't refuse. Instead, the edges of her lips curled up in a smile, and she placed her gloved hand in his.

"You're about to cause a scene," she told him in a singsong voice under her breath.

Asking her to dance at Meredith's country house party was one thing. Asking her to dance in front of all of London's finest was quite another. And they both knew it.

"That's the idea," he drawled, giving her a wicked grin.

He led her onto the dance floor, and as the music swelled, they moved together, perfectly in sync.

And just as he expected—just as he *hoped*—the room gasped.

A scandalous woman and a notorious rake dancing together in full view of the *ton*? It was enough to make dowagers clutch their diamonds and debutantes widen their eyes in shock.

Clare shot him a glare. "You just ruined your reputation, Lord Trentham."

Ash smirked. "I think my reputation was ruined a long time ago."

She exhaled sharply and shook her head at him. "What *are* you doing?"

"Something reckless," he admitted. "And I'm not done yet." He leaned down to whisper in her ear, causing even more gasps from the partygoers on the sidelines. "Meet me on the balcony in an hour."

She narrowed her eyes. "Ash—"

"One hour, Clare," he murmured as the dance ended, brushing his lips over her knuckles as he let go of her hand. "Don't make me wait."

Before she could refuse, he turned and walked away.

AN HOUR LATER, Ash stood on the Merriweathers' balcony, the cool night air doing nothing to settle the riot inside him.

This was it.

He was about to change his life. The other night, he hadn't truly asked her…not properly. Tonight, he intended to change that. To show her that he meant it. To make her believe they could have a life together. A real one. A happy one.

He had no idea how she would respond, but he had to try. Clare was the only woman who had ever made him want more, and if she told him no—*God help him*—he didn't know what he'd do.

The door to the balcony opened, and he heard the rustle of skirts behind him. He turned, his heart pounding.

But it wasn't Clare.

Instead, Lady Julia Fairbanks stepped forward, her expression coy yet somehow equally calculated.

"Lord Trentham," she purred, stepping much too close. "What a *coincidence*, finding you out here alone."

Ash resisted the urge to groan. "It's not a coincidence, is it?"

She smiled prettily, ignoring his pointed tone. "A man like you shouldn't be alone at a ball. Not when there are so many *eager* unmarried ladies about."

Bloody hell.

He took a step back, but before he could send her on her way, the sound of approaching footsteps made Ash's breath catch in his throat.

Someone was coming.

Ash knew what would happen next. What this *looked like* —him alone on a balcony with an unmarried female. The very trap he had spent years avoiding. And Lady Julia had clearly planned it. No doubt it was her mother or some equally loquacious dowager set to call the alarm.

But just as he was about to close his eyes and groan in abject misery, *Clare* stepped forward onto the balcony, her presence shattering the charged silence between him and Lady Julia.

Julia turned, her expression shifting from surprise to irritation. "Oh, how lovely," she snapped. "The ever-watchful Lady Clare, skulking about where she doesn't belong."

Clare returned Julia's sneer with a falsely sweet smile. "Oh, I belong wherever I choose, Lady Julia. It's *you* who seems to be lost."

Julia's eyes narrowed to slits. "Run along, Clare. This doesn't concern you."

Clare tilted her head, feigning curiosity. "No? Because from where I'm standing, it looks rather like you're trying to force a proposal." She glanced at Ash, who was watching this unfold, torn between astonishment, relief, and amusement. "And if that's the case, I think I'll stay."

Before Julia could deliver a retort, a voice rang out from the doorway.

"Julia?" Lady Fairbanks's sharp tone cut through the air. Lady Merriweather stood beside her, eyes widening at the sight of the three of them.

Damn.

And in that moment, without hesitation, Clare stepped forward, grabbed Ash's lapels, and pulled him into an openmouthed kiss.

His body went rigid for a fraction of a second, then his hands caught her waist, steadying her. The world faded, the scandalized gasps from the doorway barely registering.

When Clare finally pulled back, her breath was uneven, but her triumphant smile was firmly in place as she turned to Julia. "Well," she whispered smoothly, "I do believe that settles it."

It took Ash another moment to catch up, but when he did, the realization hit him like a blow.

Clare had just ruined herself—again—to save him from being forced to marry Julia.

There was no turning back now.

CHAPTER THIRTY-SEVEN

Everything was a blur.

The moment the rumors started, whispers swept through the ballroom like wildfire. At some point, Meredith grabbed Clare by the wrist and all but dragged her out. Griffin had been close behind, throwing a sharp glare at anyone who dared to stare too long.

Meredith hadn't allowed Ash to travel with them. She needed time to speak with Clare, she told him. *Alone.*

Now, in the dim candlelight of the carriage, Clare sat frozen, her pulse still pounding from the sheer madness of what had just happened.

She had done it.

She had ruined herself. *Again.*

But this time, it wasn't with some worthless rake who had discarded her like an afterthought.

This time, it was with Ash.

And there was no regret.

But she'd never seen Meredith so flustered.

"What were you thinking?" Meredith asked, her pale palms pressed to her flushed cheeks.

Clare let out a harsh breath, smoothing her temples with her fingers. "I wasn't exactly thinking."

"Don't worry," Meredith said, reaching over to squeeze Clare's cold hand. "We'll handle this. We'll figure something out. We'll—"

Griffin, seated across from them, blew out a deep breath. "Will we?" He sounded skeptical.

Meredith shot him a glare. "*Not* helping."

Clare barely heard them.

Her mind was already racing ahead.

Her mother.

Her mother was going to *lose her mind.*

If Mama had been furious over Marsden, this would send her *straight* into hysterics. She had always threatened to send Clare away, to lock her in a convent where she couldn't embarrass the family name any further.

And this?

This was enough to have her packed off to the nuns before *breakfast.*

Unless…

Her heart began to hammer. *Unless she left first.* She could still sneak off to Paris. Slip away tonight while Mama was sleeping. With Meredith and Griffin's help this time.

Clare lifted her chin. "I need to leave."

Meredith's brows snapped together. "What?"

"I need to leave London," she said, her voice steadier now. "Before Mama discovers what happened."

Meredith's eyes widened. "*What?* Clare, you can't just—"

"I can," she cut in, nodding. "And I will."

Griffin studied her for a long moment, his expression unreadable. "Is that what you *want*, Clare?"

She knew he wasn't just asking about her decision—he was asking about Ash. If she wanted to stay for him. But her feelings hadn't changed. Yes, she had saved Ash from Lady Julia, but that didn't mean she intended to marry him.

She hadn't wanted to marry him out of pity. She certainly wasn't about to do so now out of *obligation*.

Clare met Griffin's gaze, her own steady and unwavering. "Yes. It's what I want."

Meredith shook her head. "But I don't understand. Where will you go?"

Clare took a slow breath, forcing down the nerves threatening to strangle her. "Paris."

She was going to Paris.

And she wasn't coming back.

CHAPTER THIRTY-EIGHT

This wasn't how it was supposed to happen. Ash had imagined something different—something grand, something unforgettable. He had planned to ask Clare to marry him on the balcony, under the stars, to drop to one knee and tell her everything in his heart. Mainly, that he was madly in love with her and could not live without her.

Instead, he was here.

At Meredith's house.

Standing in the middle of the drawing room in the middle of the night, disheveled and exhausted, staring at the only woman who had ever mattered to him.

Clare looked at him like she was already halfway gone. "I'm leaving," she said, her voice flat. "Tonight."

Panic gripped him. *No.*

Without thinking, he sank to one knee, pulling the ring he'd procured from the jeweler earlier in the week from his pocket—the one he had carried to the ball, waiting for the right moment. "*Please* marry me."

The words hung in the air, sharp and undeniable.

Clare sucked in a breath, her eyes widening. But then, just as quickly, her expression hardened. "No."

Ash blinked. "What?"

She crossed her arms over her chest. "No."

He shot to his feet and scrubbed a hand through his hair. "Why not?"

"Because I know why you're doing this," she snapped.

His jaw clenched. "Oh, really? Enlighten me."

She lifted her chin, a defiant fire in her eyes. "You think this will fix everything. You think proposing will make the scandal disappear. That it'll *save* me. Well, what if I don't want to be saved?" Fire flashed in her eyes.

Ash stared at her, stunned. "You think I want to marry you out of *duty*?"

She let out a sharp, humorless laugh. "I know you do."

His heart pounded. His hands curled into fists at his sides. "What if I told you I love you?"

Clare went still. The silence between them stretched long and unbearable.

Then, finally, she spoke, her voice quieter now. "I'd tell you that you're…you're a fool." But she glanced away.

A sharp pain twisted in his chest.

She meant it.

She *truly* believed he was only here out of obligation. That he didn't mean it. That what they had meant nothing.

His fingers twitched at his sides, itching to hold her, to make her see. But she was already shaking her head. "I'm leaving for Paris."

His breath caught. "Clare—"

"Good-bye, Ash."

She said it so firmly, so finally, that he felt it like a blow. She wanted him gone. And if she had to break him to make it happen, so be it.

She turned without another word, her skirts swishing as she walked toward the door.

He should stop her. He should fight for her.

But he didn't.

Because for the first time in his life, he didn't know how to win.

So he watched her go.

And if this was what love felt like, it could go straight to hell.

CHAPTER THIRTY-NINE

The night was suffocating. Clare sat alone in the dim candlelight of her bedchamber, staring blankly at the packed trunk by the door. She had planned everything—her escape, her future, her refusal to let a man decide her fate ever again.

So why did it feel like her chest was caving in?

She wrapped her arms around herself, as if that would stop the ache spreading through her ribs.

She *was* doing the right thing.

She had to keep telling herself that.

Ash had only proposed because of duty, because of guilt, because he thought she needed saving.

And she wouldn't let him be trapped like that.

Not with her.

Because she already knew—*knew*—what it felt like to be unwanted. And she had no intention of spending a lifetime with that feeling.

But then, as she sat there, breathing through the hollow emptiness, a strange unease unfurled in her stomach, something deeper than heartbreak, something physical.

She had felt…different. For days now.

She closed her eyes, counted back the weeks in her head.

Her stomach clenched.

No.

Her breath came faster, shallower.

No, no, no.

It couldn't be.

Her hands trembled as she pressed them against her abdomen, as if she could *feel* the truth lying beneath her skin.

Ash.

She had left him. Pushed him away. Broken both their hearts.

And now—*now*—she suspected she was carrying his child. Tears burned at the corners of her eyes, but she refused to let them fall.

Because this changed everything.

And at the same time, it changed nothing.

She was still leaving. She had to.

Even if it meant carrying this secret with her all the way to Paris.

CHAPTER FORTY

One Hour Later

Ash sat in his sister's drawing room, staring into the fire, a glass of brandy untouched in his hand.

He had lost her.

Clare had already left, and there was nothing he could do about it. Because she had made it clear. She didn't want him. And the worst part? She thought he had only proposed out of duty.

Bloody hell.

Hadn't he spent his entire life avoiding marriage for that very reason? Avoiding being trapped? Avoiding falling in love?

But now, sitting here, gut-punched and hollow, he finally understood. It had never been about duty. It had never been about saving her reputation.

It had been about her.

Because he was in love with her.

And he had let her walk away.

"You're an idiot." Meredith's voice cut through the silence, sharp and unimpressed.

Ash exhaled through his nose, not bothering to look at her. "Good evening to you too, dear sister."

She folded her arms, standing over him like a particularly disapproving angel of doom. "You let her go."

His jaw clenched. "She didn't want me."

Meredith scoffed. "Oh, please. She didn't want to be an obligation. And instead of proving that she wasn't, you just let her run off."

He finally looked at her, scowling. "What the hell else was I supposed to do? I asked her to *marry* me. I got down on *one knee*, for heaven's sake."

Meredith's eyes flashed. "How about fight for her?"

Ash opened his mouth—ready to argue, ready to explain why it was too late.

"She's pregnant," Meredith added quietly.

Silence.

A long, stretched-out, gut-wrenching silence while Ash's brain struggled to make sense of those two overwhelming words.

Then…

"What?"

Meredith rolled her eyes. "Oh, don't look at me like that. You heard me. She told me just before she left. She begged me not to tell you, but you two have made such an absolute mess of things that I have no choice but to intervene." Meredith shook her head, exasperated. "I've been watching, waiting, *hoping* you would fall in love and marry like *normal* people. But apparently, that's far too simple for the two of you."

She huffed. "I hid a letter in Clare's valise because she *insisted* on leaving before her mother wakes up. But I'm here to tell you to your face—you're an idiot, and if you don't go after her right now, you'll regret it for the rest of your life. Now, go. Fight for her." She pointed toward the door.

Ash's heartbeat thundered in his ears. He'd heard what his sister said, but he remained focused on one word. And one word alone.

Pregnant.

Clare was pregnant.

With his child.

Something visceral took hold of him, something he couldn't name—possessive, protective, overwhelming.

He shot to his feet. "Why the hell didn't she tell me?"

"Because she's stubborn and scared and convinced you only proposed because of the scandal," Meredith snapped. "And considering how you let her go without a fight, I can't exactly blame her."

Ash dragged a hand through his hair, his mind spinning. "I—"

"No," Meredith cut him off. "You don't get to stand here and wallow in self-pity. You love her. You *love* her. Griffin already told me, so don't try to deny it. Just go and prove it to her, you fool."

Ash swallowed hard. He lowered his voice to a whisper. "I would never deny it."

Meredith's face softened. She stepped toward him and put a hand on his shoulder. "You're scared too. I know that. *And* I know why. You've always been afraid that you'd end up alone like Father. And if you did it by choice, you could say you wanted it." She gave him a wry smile. "But you're a good man, Ash. You're nothing like Father was. And you deserve all the love and happiness in this world."

Ash's chin quivered. He couldn't help it. "When did you become so astute, Mere?"

Meredith smiled and tipped her head back and forth. "Probably about the time you gave me a similar speech, telling me what a fool I was for pushing Griffin away." Her smile widened. "I believe you even called me a *hypocritical fool*."

Ash bowed his head and scratched the back of his neck. Then he winced. "*Mmm*. I did, didn't I?"

"Yes, you did. And I would not be the sister you need if I didn't return the favor now. Go after her, Ash. You'll know what to say to convince her you love her."

Ash expelled his breath. Meredith was right. He was scared. Scared out of his wits, really. All of this was new to him. He'd never been in love before, and for the first time in his life, he *wanted* marriage.

Not because he had to. Not because it was expected. Not even because Clare was carrying his child. It was more than that.

He wanted her because he couldn't live without her.

His fists tightened at his sides. No more hesitating. No more doubting. He had wasted enough time.

It was time to convince her.

CHAPTER FORTY-ONE

The carriage rattled over the uneven road, the rhythmic clatter of wheels on cobblestones a steady reminder that she was *leaving*.

London was behind her. *Ash* was behind her. And soon, she would be in Paris.

Alone…well, *nearly* alone.

She glanced at her maid who sat across from her, her head propped against the side of the coach, gently snoring. Then she pressed a hand to her stomach, still flat, still unchanged, but no less real. Her secret. Her future.

Meredith had tried to talk her out of leaving, of course. For a moment Clare had worried her friend might try to lock her in her bedchamber. But in the end, Clare had convinced Mere that she was a grown woman who had made her decision.

She probably shouldn't have told Meredith she suspected she was with child. Meredith was rubbish at keeping secrets. But she'd had to tell *someone*, and if she was honest with herself, some small part of her realized that Ash deserved to know.

Then she'd gone, with her maid, and her trunk, and her valise. Griffin had insisted on hiring a coach to take them safely to Calais. And with each rotation of the wagon's wheels, Clare had told herself this was the only way. That she had done the right thing.

So why did it feel like she had left a piece of herself behind?

She sighed. There was no way she could sleep. Perhaps she would read by the candlelight. She leaned down to rummage in the valise at her feet and found…a letter.

It was folded and sealed and addressed to her. Frowning, she sat back in the seat and opened it.

It was from Meredith.

Dearest Clare,

We have been friends for over a decade, so I do hope you will not take offense when I tell you that you are being an idiot.

Honestly, for someone as intelligent as you are, you're proving to be a true mess when it comes to love. But then again, I suppose we all are. Including my fool of a brother.

CLARE BIT HER LIP. Meredith knew? What else did she know? She eagerly continued reading.

I know you both thought you were fooling

me, but I've had my suspicions ever since Ash asked you to dance at the house party. And, by the by, if anything more than that went on between you, ahem, suffice it to say, I don't care to know the details.

Regardless of how you got here, it is obvious to Griffin and myself that you and Ash have fallen in love. And I know you well enough to know that you are going to think all sorts of outlandish thoughts about it because that is your nature.

Had you seen fit to ask my counsel, I wouldn't have to write this letter and send it off with you in the middle of the night. Yet here we are. And it's time for me to tell you some rather difficult truths.

CLARE HELD HER BREATH. Did she dare continue reading? Of course she had to.

Marsden was an ass who never deserved you. And as far as I'm concerned, your hideous mother was to blame for making you so desperate to leave her house, you made a huge mistake that changed the course of your life.

But don't you see?

You have another chance now. You have a chance at true love. A love based on shared interests, shared history, a shared sense of humor, and—dare I say it?—shared wounds.

Because as much as I love my brother, I know his faults. Due to his treatment at the hands of our father, Ash turned off his emotions at a young age. He substituted charming smiles and delightful jests for anything of real substance. It's truly broken my heart all these years to watch him flit from one meaningless affair to the next, never allowing his heart to become involved.

But with you it's different, Clare. I've never seen Ash act the way he does around you. I've never seen him look at anyone the way he looks at you. You and Ash have the chance for a love that is rarely written about in sonnets. It's not the kind of love that merely brings you flowers or kisses you softly on the cheek. It's the kind of love that knows what you've been through and loves you all the more for it.

TEARS STREAMED DOWN Clare's face, and she wiped them away with her fingers. She sucked in a breath. She had to finish reading.

By now, I hope I've made my point and that you're prepared to stop your flight, turn around and come back, and live the life you are clearly meant to. I am about to go downstairs and say very similar things to my idiot brother, and if I am any sort of persuasive speaker, he may arrive at any moment...

Your future sister-in-law and current closest friend,

Meredith

TEARS CONTINUED to stream down Clare's face, plopping onto the pages and smearing the ink. She understood what Meredith was saying, the part of her letter that wasn't even there. Fear. It was fear keeping Clare from opening up her heart to Ash. Fear of being rejected again and fear of being too happy because happiness was such an unfamiliar emotion to her.

But Meredith was perfectly right, of course. She and Ash had a shared history, a shared sense of humor, shared interests, and shared desires. Soon, they would even share a child.

It was safe. It was safe to be loved and to love and to accept a life filled with happiness. That's what Meredith was saying. And Clare needed to get back immediately and begin her future.

She knocked on the carriage roof just as it was beginning to slow. She frowned, sitting forward as the driver called out in frustration. There was something in the road ahead.

Or rather—*someone.*

The door flung open, and before Clare could react, a familiar figure climbed inside.

Ash.

Breathless. Wild-eyed. *Gorgeous.*

Her heart stopped.

Sparing a quick glance at the still sleeping maid, he dropped onto the seat next to Clare, his chest rising and falling, his cravat loose, his hair mussed. The man looked as if he had been riding for hours.

"What— What are you doing?" she gasped, searching his beloved face.

He threw something onto her lap, still attempting to catch his breath.

She glanced down at it. A diamond.

The biggest, most ridiculous, obscene diamond ring she had ever seen. She hadn't looked at it earlier. She'd been too focused on refusing him.

"Marry me," he said, voice hoarse, urgent. "Please."

Clare stared at him, stunned.

"Ash—"

"I don't care where we live," he went on, rushing the words, as if afraid she would bolt out the other side of the carriage. "Paris, London, the bloody countryside—it doesn't matter. I just need you."

Her throat tightened.

"I know you're pregnant," he admitted, softer now. "But that's not why I'm here." His voice turned raw. "I love you, Clare. *Not* because of duty. *Not* because of obligation. Just because you're you. I love you beyond all reason and all measure, and I think I have since the night you stole into Southbury's study in search of brandy."

Tears blurred her vision. For so long, she had convinced herself that no one would ever love her like this. That she wasn't meant for happy endings.

But here he was.

Begging.

Loving her regardless.

She covered her mouth with her hands, overwhelmed.

"Say something," Ash murmured, still searching her face, almost pleading.

Clare launched herself forward, wrapped her arms around his neck, and kissed him. It wasn't graceful. It wasn't soft. It was desperate, wild, and full of every emotion she had buried since the moment she had walked away. "I love you too," she breathed against his lips.

"Does that mean you'll marry me?"

"Yes," she said, crying tears of joy this time. "Yes, I shall marry you."

"Finally," he groaned, pulling her closer, one hand tangled in her hair, the other settling against her hip.

When they pulled apart, she pressed her forehead to his, breathless. How in the world was her maid sleeping through all of this? She suspected the girl was merely pretending at this point, but she was too happy to care.

"I have been miserable without you," he whispered.

"All two hours of it?" she said with a wry smile.

"All two," he replied, nodding.

"Meredith is rubbish at keeping secrets," she added next.

"She's also not the most careful speaker. She called me an idiot more than once."

Clare giggled. "She called me an idiot too."

He pressed his head to her forehead again. "You're not an idiot, love, but *you are so damn stubborn*." He chuckled, though his voice was thick with emotion.

She smiled. "But you like that about me, don't you?" She gave him a saucy wink.

"I like *everything* about you," he said before pulling her close again for another kiss.

EPILOGUE

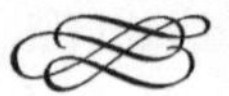

One Year Later, The Duke of Southbury's Town House

Clare and Ash, Gemma and Lucian, and Meredith and Griffin all sat in the drawing room of Griffin's town house. Their babies, so near in age, were all settled on their father's laps.

"Who would have ever thought the three of you would be such devoted fathers?" Meredith said, shaking her head as she looked about the room.

"Are you quite serious?" Griffin replied, looking affronted. "I have been waiting to meet our son for *far* too long." He bounced the baby on his knee, smiling at him with a ridiculously proud look upon his face.

"I'm telling you, Southbury," Ash interjected, "you'll want a daughter as soon as possible. I am in love with mine." He stared down at the little girl who lay cuddled in his arms, rubbing a fingertip tenderly over her tiny, soft cheek.

"I second that," Lucian said from his seat across from the settee. "I am *thrilled* to have a daughter." He leaned down and kissed his baby's forehead. "She's absolutely gorgeous and will be even more so when she comes of age," he finished with a wink at his wife.

"You'll have to beat the suitors away with a stick," Gemma replied to her husband, laughing.

"Speaking of beating someone," Meredith interjected, clearing her throat and arching a brow. "How's the Earl of Marsden doing?"

The three gentlemen gave each other knowing glances.

"Ahem, I hear his ribs are nearly healed," Ash said, the hint of a smile on his lips.

"His broken nose may take a bit longer," Griffin added, poking out his cheek with his tongue.

"Perhaps even longer than his broken arm?" Lucian speculated.

Clare shook her head and rolled her eyes. Soon after she'd returned to town with Ash, he had challenged Lord Marsden to a boxing match. Only he'd failed to inform the good earl of just how talented a boxer he happened to be.

The entire *ton* had purchased tickets to the event. For seeing the new husband of the previously scorned Lady Clare in hand-to-hand combat with the man who'd ruined her was far too tempting a spectacle to ignore. Apparently, it was the most well attended match the boxing saloon had ever seen.

And it did not disappoint. By the time the fight was through, Lord Marsden was a bloody heap. A doctor had been called to see to him, and it was reported in the papers later that a spectator had clearly heard Lord Trentham say to his downed opponent in a scathing voice, "*That* was for Clare."

As for the papers, they had done a magnificent job of turning Clare and Ash's hasty marriage into a Society event instead of a scandal broth. Clare had ensured the correct rumors were whispered into the correct ears and in very little time, she and Ash had gone from the biggest scandal in an age to the most coveted couple on any hostess's list of invitees.

Funny how a respectable marriage to a marquess could change a lady's fortunes. These days, both she and Ash continued to do whatever they pleased, and the silly *ton* couldn't seem to get enough of it. They were *such* a fickle lot.

But the *ton*'s about-face was *not* Clare's favorite thing that had happened after she agreed to marry Ash.

Her *very* favorite thing was Ash's discussion with her mother when they made it back to Meredith's town house. Nearly the moment they'd stepped through the door, he'd pulled Mama aside to speak with her privately in the drawing room.

Of course, Clare and Meredith had pressed their ears to the door to hear every word. And what a discussion it had been. Ash had begun by quickly giving Mama a rundown of what had happened at the Merriweathers' ball. Then Mama, loud with hysterics, had claimed she needed smelling salts.

"Quick, get the salts," Meredith had ordered a maid who had just happened by.

At Clare's questioning look, she'd explained that she wanted to ensure that Clare's mother remained perfectly awake and alert to hear every single word Ash had to say to her.

Mama had not fainted, of course, but there had been a great deal of dramatics that Ash mostly ignored while he informed her that he had offered for Clare, Clare had accepted, and they were to be married immediately as soon as Ash procured a special license. He further informed her mother that she had best not say so much as one unkind word to Clare for the rest of her days or she would have to answer to her soon-to-be new son-in-law.

Clare's eyes had filled with tears as she listened to Ash

defend her so valiantly. "You didn't deserve to be Clare's mother," Ash had said. "But sometimes life gives us parents who are less than ideal. What's done is done. But I will be her husband soon, and I intend to take better care of her for the rest of her life than you ever did."

At that, Meredith had clasped her hands together over her heart and let out a loud, long sigh. "Oh, he's wonderful, isn't he?" Meredith said.

"So very wonderful," Clare agreed, dabbing at her eyes with her handkerchief.

By the time Ash and Mama emerged from the drawing room, Mama did little more than nod at Clare as she walked past before issuing a curt, "Congratulations on your impending nuptials." Then she went directly to her room to pack.

Ash stepped out of the room. "I invited her to the wedding," he informed the two ladies, who were forced to suddenly act as if they had some sort of business standing in the corridor directly outside the drawing room. "But she's leaving for the country directly after."

"Not a moment too soon," Meredith replied before she and Clare had both burst out laughing. They couldn't help themselves.

Now, as they all sat in Southbury's drawing room together, Clare glanced around at her friends. "I truly marvel at what a difference a year has made in my life," she told them all. "Instead of being alone, I have a marvelous husband and a beautiful daughter, friends, family, and a wonderful life full of love and happiness. And I have all of you to thank for it."

"We're happy to have you as one of us," Meredith replied with a bright smile. "And as for the difference a year makes, you've gone from the infamous Scandalton to the beloved Marchioness of Trentham."

"Oh, the *ton* is not so clever," Clare replied. "After all, I spent years learning how rumors turn possibilities into reality. I always knew how to turn the tide. I suppose I never really wanted to."

"Until you fell in love with me?" Ash interjected, giving her a loving smile.

"Until I fell in love with you," Clare agreed, returning his smile.

"I can vouch for that," Gemma interjected. "The rumors of our divorce nearly disappeared overnight after Clare got involved." She exchanged a glance with her husband.

"Yes. You know, that is quite a skill you have with public opinion," Meredith said to Clare, tapping a finger against her cheek. "You should really use it more often."

"Actually, I intend to," Clare replied. "Just last week, I was approached by one of the debutantes." She gave them all a sly smile. "She's asked for my assistance."

"Ooh, assistance with what? Do tell," Gemma said, waggling her brows.

"It seems the wallflowers are planning a revolt," Clare announced. "And *I* am going to help them."

Want one more wicked night with Clare and Ash?
CLICK HERE for a steamy bonus scene and to join my
newsletter…as the scandalous marchioness and her devoted
marquess return to the Onyx Club—one year of marriage,
one locked room, and absolutely no intention of behaving
or type
https://dl.bookfunnel.com/1gi4o75st6
into your browser.

Thank you for reading *The Marquess Match*. If you enjoyed it, I would truly appreciate your recommendations and reviews. Want more?

CLICK HERE to read The Wallflower's Great Escape, the first book in the related Wallflowers' Revolt trilogy, where one runaway wallflower, one unwanted marriage, and one infuriatingly handsome brother's best friend collide in the most deliciously scandalous way.

And Clare Handleton? She's there too—putting her talents as a scandal-fixer to excellent use as she helps a new band of wallflowers take on Society itself.

The Unlikely Lady (Book 3)

The Irresistible Rogue (Book 4)

The Unforgettable Hero (Book 4.5)

The Untamed Earl (Book 5)

The Legendary Lord (Book 6)

Never Trust a Pirate (Book 7)

The Right Kind of Rogue (Book 8)

A Duke Like No Other (Book 9)

Kiss Me At Christmas (Book 10)

Mr. Hunt, I Presume (Book 10.5)

No Other Duke But You (Book 11)

Secret Brides

Secrets of a Wedding Night (Book 1)

A Secret Proposal (Book 1.5)

Secrets of a Runaway Bride (Book 2)

A Secret Affair (Book 2.5)

Secrets of a Scandalous Marriage (Book 3)

It Happened Under the Mistletoe (Book 3.5)

Thank you for reading *The Marquess Match.* I hope you enjoyed Clare and Ash's story.

I'd love to keep in touch.

- Visit my website for exclusive information about upcoming books, excerpts, and to sign up for my email newsletter: www.ValerieBowmanBooks.com or at www.ValerieBowmanBooks.com/subscribe.
- Join me on Facebook: http://Facebook.com/ValerieBowmanAuthor.
- Join me on Instagram: http://www.instagram.com/valeriegbowman/
- Reviews help other readers find books. I appreciate all reviews. Thank you so much for considering it!

Want to read the other Love's a Game books?

- The Duchess Hunt
- The Duke Dare

ABOUT THE AUTHOR

Valerie Bowman grew up in Illinois with six sisters (she's number seven) and a huge supply of romance novels.

After a cold and snowy stint earning a degree in English with a minor in history at Smith College, she moved to Florida the first chance she got.

Valerie now lives in Jacksonville with her family including her two rascally dogs. When she's not writing, she keeps busy reading, traveling, or vacillating between watching crazy reality TV and PBS.

Valerie loves to hear from readers. Find her on the web at www.ValerieBowmanBooks.com.

facebook.com/ValerieBowmanAuthor

instagram.com/valeriegbowman

goodreads.com/Valerie_Bowman

bookbub.com/authors/valerie-bowman

amazon.com/author/valeriebowman